The Merry-Go-Round

Carl Van Vechten

Contents

THE MERRY-GO-ROUND

BY

Carl Van Vechten

The
Merry-Go-Round

Carl Van Vechten

"Tournez, tournez, bons chevaux de bois,
  Tournez cent tours, tournez mille tours,
  Tournez souvent et tournez toujours,
  Tournez, tournez au sons de hautbois."

PAUL VERLAINE

Some of these essays have appeared in "The Smart Set,"
"Reedy's Mirror," "Vanity Fair," "The Chronicle," "The
Theatre," "The Bellman," "The Musical Quarterly," "Rogue,"
"The New York Press," and "The New York Globe." In their
present form, however, they have undergone considerable
redressing.

In Defence of Bad Taste

"It is a painful thing, at best, to live up to one's
bricabric, if one has any; but to live up to the bricabric
of many lands and of many centuries is a strain which no
wise man would dream of inflicting upon his constitution."

Agnes Repplier.

In Defence of Bad Taste

In America, where men are supposed to know nothing about matters of
taste and where women have their dresses planned for them, the
household decorator has become an important factor in domestic life.
Out of an even hundred rich men how many can say that they have had
anything to do with the selection or arrangement of the furnishings
for their homes? In theatre programs these matters are regulated and
due credit is given to the various firms who have supplied the myriad
appeals to the eye; one knows who thought out the combinations of
shoes, hats, and parasols, and one knows where each separate article
was purchased. Why could not some similar plan of appreciation be
followed in the houses of our very rich? Why not, for instance, a card
in the hall something like the following:

This house was furnished and decorated according
to the taste of Marcel of the Dilly-Billy Shop

or

> We are living in the kind of house Miss Simone
> O'Kelly thought we should live in. The
> decorations are pure Louis XV and
> the furniture is authentic.

It is not difficult, of course, to differentiate the personal from the impersonal. Nothing clings so ill to the back as borrowed finery and I have yet to find the family which has settled itself fondly and comfortably in chairs which were a part of some one else's aesthetic plan. As a matter of fact many of our millionaires would be more at home in an atmosphere concocted from the ingredients of plain pine tables and blanket-covered mattresses than they are surrounded by the frippery of China and the frivolity of France. If these gentlemen were fortunate enough to enjoy sufficient confidence in their own taste to give it a thorough test it is not safe to think of the extreme burden that would be put on the working capacity of the factories of the Grand Rapids furniture companies. We might find a few emancipated souls scouring the town for heavy refectory tables and divans into which one could sink, reclining or upright, with a perfect sense of ease, but these would be as rare as Steinway pianos in Coney Island.

For Americans are meek in such matters. They credit themselves with no taste. They fear comparison. If the very much sought-after Simone O'Kelly has decorated Mr. B.'s house Mr. M. does not dare to struggle along with merely his own ideas in furnishing his. He calls in an expert who begins, rather inauspiciously, by painting the dining-room salmon pink. The tables and chairs will be made by somebody on Tenth Street, exact copies of a set to be found in the Musee Carnavalet. The legs under the table are awkwardly arranged for diners but they look very well when the table is unclothed. The decorator plans to hang Mr. M.'s personal bedroom in pale plum colour. Mr. M. rebels at this. "I detest," he remarks mildly, "all variants of purple." "Very well," acquiesces the decorator, "we will make it green." In the end Mr. M.'s worst premonitions are realized: the walls are resplendent in a striking shade of magenta. Along the edge of each panel of Chinese brocade a narrow band of absinthe velvet ribbon gives the necessary contrast. The furniture is painted in dull ivory with touches of gold and beryl and the bed cover is peacock blue. Four round cushions of a similar shade repose on the floor at the foot of the bed. The fat manufacturer's wife as she enters this triumph of decoration which might satisfy Louise de la Valliere or please Doris Keane, is an anachronistic figure and she is aware of it. She prefers, on the whole, the brass bedsteads of the summer hotels. Mr. M. himself feels ridiculous. He never enters the room without a groan and a remark on the order of "Good God, what a colour!" His personal taste finds its supreme enjoyment in the Circassian walnut panelling, desk, and tables of the directors' room in the Millionaire's Trust and Savings Bank. "Rich and tasteful": how many times he has used this phrase to express his approval! In the mid-Victorian red plush of his club, too, he is comfortable. "Waiter, another whiskey and soda!"

Mildred is expected home after her first year in boarding school. Her mother wishes to environ her, so to speak. Mildred is delicate in her tastes, so delicate that she scarcely ever expresses herself. Her mind and body are pure; her heart beats faster when she learns of distress. Voluptuousness, Venus, and Vice are all merely words to her. Mother does not explain this to the decorator. "My daughter is returning from school," she says, "I want her room done." "What style of room?" "After all you are supposed to know that. I am engaging you to arrange it for me." "Your daughter, I take it, is a modern girl?" "You may assume as much." In despair for a hint the decorator steals a look at a photograph of the miss, full-lipped, melting dark eyes, and blue-black hair. Sensing an houri he hangs the walls with a deep shade of Persian orange, over which flit tropical birds of emerald and

azure; strange pomegranates bleed their seeds at regular intervals.
The couch is an adaptation, in colour, of the celebrated ***Sumurun***
bed. The dressing table and the ***chaise-longue*** are of Chinese
lacquer. A heavy bronze incense burner pours forth fumes of Bichara's
Scheherazade. From the window frames, stifling the light, depend
flame-coloured brocaded curtains embroidered in Egyptian enamelled
beads. It is a triumph, this chamber, of ***style Ballet Russe***. Diana
is banished ... and shrinking Mildred, returning from school, finds
her demure soul at variance with her surroundings.

A man's house should be the expression of the man himself. All the
books on the subject and even the household decorators themselves will
tell you that. But, if the decoration of a house is to express its
owner, it is necessary that he himself inspire it, which implies, of
course, the possession of ideas, even though they be bad. And men in
these United States are not expected to display mental anguish or
pleasure when confronted by colour combinations. In America one is
constantly hearing young ladies say, "He's a man and so, of course,
knows nothing about colour," or "Of course a man never looks at
clothes." It does not seem to be necessary to argue this point. One
has only to remember that Veronese was a man; so was Velasquez. Even
Paul Poiret and Leon Bakst belong to the sex of Adam. Nevertheless
most Americans still consider it a little ***effemine***, a trifle
declasse, for a business man (allowances are sometimes made for
poets, musicians, actors, and people who live in Greenwich Village),
to make any references to colour or form. He may admire, with obvious
emphasis on the women they lightly enclose, the costumes of the
Follies but he is not permitted to exhibit knowledge of materials
and any suddenly expressed desire on his part to rush into a shop and
hug some bit of colour from the show window to his heart would be
regarded as a symptom of madness.

The audience which gives the final verdict on a farce makes allowances for the author; permits him the use of certain conventions. For example, he is given leave to introduce a hotel corridor into his last act with seven doors opening on a common hallway so that his characters may conveniently and persistently enter the wrong rooms. It may be supposed that I ask for some such license from my audience. "How ridiculous," you may be saying, "I know of interior decorators who spend weeks in reading out the secrets of their clients' souls in order to provide their proper settings." There doubtless are interior decorators who succeed in giving a home the appearance of a well-kept hotel where guests may mingle comfortably and freely. I should not wish to deny this. But I do deny that soul-study is a requirement for the profession. If a man (or a woman) has a soul it will not be a decorator who will discover its fitting housing. Others may object, "But bad taste is rampant. Surely it is better to be guided by some one who knows than to surround oneself with rocking chairs, plaster casts of the Winged Victory, and photographs of various madonnas." I say that it is *not* better. It is better for each man to express himself, through his taste, as well as through his tongue or his pen, as he may. And it is only through such expression that he will finally arrive (if he ever can) at a condition of household furnishing which will say something to his neighbour as well as to himself. It is a pleasure when one leaves a dinner party to be able to observe "That is *his* house," just as it is a pleasure when one leaves a concert to remember that a composer has expressed himself and not the result of seven years study in Berlin or Paris.

But Americans have little aptitude for self-expression. They prefer to huddle, like cattle, under unspeakable whips when matters of art are under discussion. They fear ridicule. As a consequence many of the richest men in this country never really live in their own homes, never are comfortable for a moment, although the walls are hung double with Fragonards and hawthorne vases stand so deep upon the tables that no space remains for the "Saturday Review" or "le Temps." And they

never, never, never, will know the pleasure which comes while
stumbling down a side street in London, or in the mouldy corners of
the Venetian ghetto, or in the Marche du Temple in Paris, or, heaven
knows, in New York, on lower Fourth Avenue, or in Chinatown, or in a
Russian brass shop on Allen Street, or in a big department store (as
often there as anywhere) in finding just the lamp for just the table
in just the corner, or in discovering a bit of brocade, perhaps the
ragged remnant of a waistcoat belonging to an aristocrat of the
Directorate, which will lighten the depths of a certain room, or a
chair which goes miraculously with a desk already possessed, or a
Chinese mirror which one had almost decided did not exist. Nor will
they ever experience the joy of sudden decision in front of a picture
by Matisse, which ends in the sale of a Delacroix. Nor can they feel
the thrill which is part of the replacing of a make-shift rug by *the*
rug of rugs (let us hope it was Solomon's!).

I know a lady in Paris whose salon presents a different aspect each
summer. Do her Picassos go, a new Spanish painter has replaced them.
Have you missed the Gibbons carving? Spanish church carving has taken
its place. "And where are your Venetian embroideries?" "I sold them to
the Marquise de V.... The money served to buy these Persian
miniatures." This lady has travelled far. She is not experimenting in
doubtful taste or bad art; she is not even experimenting in her own
taste: she is simply enjoying different epochs, different artists,
different forms of art, each in its turn, for so long as it says
anything to her. Her house is not a museum. Space and comfort demand
exclusion but she excludes nothing forever that she desires.... She
exchanges.

Taste at best is relative. It is an axiom that anybody else's taste
can never say anything to you although you may feel perfectly certain
that it is better than your own. If more of the money of the rich
were spent in encouraging children to develop their own ideas in

furnishing their own rooms it would serve a better purpose than it does now when it is dropped into the ample pockets of the professional decorators. Oscar Wilde wrote, "A colour sense is more important in the development of the individual than a sense of right and wrong." Any young boy or girl can learn something about such matters; most of them, if not shamed out of it, take a natural interest in their surroundings. You will see how true this is if you attempt to rearrange a child's room. Those who have bad taste, relatively, should literally be allowed to make their own beds. On the whole it is preferable to be comfortable in red and green velvet upholstery than to be beautiful and unhappy in a household decorator's gilded cage.

September 3, 1915.

Music and Supermusic

"To know whether you are enjoying a piece of music or not you must see whether you find yourself looking at the advertisements of Pears' soap at the end of the program."

Samuel Butler.

Music and Supermusic

What is the distinction in the mind of Everycritic between good music

and bad music, in the mind of Everyman between popular music and
"classical" music? What is the essential difference between an air by
Mozart and an air by Jerome Kern? Why is Chopin's **G minor nocturne**
better music than Thecla Badarzewska's **La Priere d'une Vierge**? Why
is a music drama by Richard Wagner preferable to a music drama by
Horatio W. Parker? What makes a melody distinguished? What makes a
melody commonplace or cheap? Why do some melodies ring in our ears
generation after generation while others enjoy but a brief popularity?
Why do certain composers, such as Raff and Mendelssohn, hailed as
geniuses while they were yet alive, soon sink into semi-obscurity,
while others, such as Robert Franz and Moussorgsky, almost
unrecognized by their contemporaries, grow in popularity? Are there no
answers to these conundrums and the thousand others that might be
asked by a person with a slight attack of curiosity?... No one **does**
ask and assuredly no one answers. These riddles, it would seem, are
included among the forbidden mysteries of the sphynx. The critics
assert with authority and some show of erudition that the Spohrs, the
Mendelssohns, the Humperdincks, and the Montemezzis are great
composers. They usually admire the grandchildren of Old Lady Tradition
but they neglect to justify this partiality. Nor can we trust the
public with its favourite Piccinnis and Puccinis.... What then is the
test of supermusic?

For we know, as well as we can know anything, that there is music and
supermusic. Rubinstein wrote music; Beethoven wrote supermusic (Mr.
Finck may contradict this statement). Bellini wrote operas; Mozart
wrote superoperas. Jensen wrote songs; Schubert wrote supersongs. The
superiority of **Voi che sapete** as a vocal melody over Ah! non
giunge is not generally contested; neither can we hesitate very long
over the question whether or not **Der Leiermann** is a better song than
Lehn' deine Wang'. Probably even Mr. Finck will admit that the
Sonata Appassionata is finer music than the most familiar portrait
(I think it is No. 22) in the **Kamennoi-Ostrow** set. But, if we agree

to put Mozart, Bach, Beethoven, Schubert, and a few others on marmorean pedestals in a special Hall of Fame (and this is a compromise on my part, at any rate, as I consider much of the music written by even these men to be below any moderately high standard), what about the rest? Mr. Finck prefers Johann Strauss to Brahms, nay more to Richard himself! He has written a whole book for no other reason, it would seem, than to prove that the author of Tod und Verklarung is a very much over-rated individual. At times sitting despondently in Carnegie Hall, I am secretly inclined to agree with him. Personally I can say that I prefer Irving Berlin's music to that of Edward MacDowell and I would like to have some one prove to me that this position is untenable.

What is the test of supermusic? I have read that fashionable music, music composed in a style welcomed and appreciated by its contemporary hearers is seldom supermusic. Yet Handel wrote fashionable music, and so much other of the music of that epoch is Handelian that it is often difficult to be sure where George Frederick left off and somebody else began. Bellini wrote fashionable music and **Norma** and **La Sonnambula** sound a trifle faded although they are still occasionally performed, but Rossini, whose only desire was to please his public, (Liszt once observed "Rossini and Co. always close with 'I remain your very humble servant'"), wrote melodies in **Il Barbiere di Siviglia** which sound as fresh to us today as they did when they were first composed. And when this prodigiously gifted musician-cook turned his back to the public to write **Guillaume Tell** he penned a work which critics have consistently told us is a masterpiece, but which is as seldom performed today as any opera of the early Nineteenth Century which occasionally gains a hearing at all. Therefor we must be wary of the old men who tell us that we shall soon tire of the music of Puccini because it is fashionable.

Popularity is scarcely a test. I have mentioned Mendelssohn. Never was

there a more popular composer, and yet aside from the violin concerto
what work of his has maintained its place in the concert repertory?
Yet Chopin, whose name is seldom absent from the program of a pianist,
was a god in his own time and the most brilliant woman of his epoch
fell in love with him, as Philip Moeller has recently reminded us in
his very amusing play. On the other hand there is the case of Robert
Franz whose songs never achieved real popularity during his lifetime,
but which are frequently, almost invariably indeed, to be found on
song recital programs today and which are more and more appreciated.
The critics are praising him, the public likes him: they buy his
songs. And there is also the case of Max Reger who was not popular, is
not popular, and never will be popular.

Can we judge music by academic standards? Certainly not. Even the
hoary old academicians themselves can answer this question correctly
if you put it in relation to any composer born before 1820. The
greatest composers have seldom respected the rules. Beethoven in his
last sonatas and string quartets slapped all the pedants in the ears;
yet I believe you will find astonishingly few rules broken by Mozart,
one of the gods in the mythology of art music, and Berlioz, who broke
all the rules, is more interesting to us today as a writer of prose
than as a writer of music.

Is simple music supermusic? Certainly not invariably. *Vedrai Carino*
is a simple tune, almost as simple as a folk-song and we set great
store by it; yet Michael William Balfe wrote twenty-seven operas
filled with similarly simple tunes and in a selective draft of
composers his number would probably be 9,768. The *Ave Maria* of
Schubert is a simple tune; so is the *Meditation* from *Thais*. Why do
we say that one is better than the other.

Or is supermusic always grand, sad, noble, or emotional? There must be
another violent head shaking here. The air from Oberon, Ocean, thou

mighty monster, is so grand that scarcely a singer can be found today capable of interpreting it, although many sopranos puff and steam through it, for all the world like pinguid gentlemen climbing the stairs to the towers of Notre Dame. The *Fifth Symphony* of Beethoven is both grand and noble; probably no one will be found who will deny that it is supermusic, but Mahler's *Symphony of the Thousand* is likewise grand and noble, and futile and bombastic to boot. Or sai chi l'onore *is a grand air, but* Robert je t'aime is equally grand in intention, at least. *Der Tod und das Madchen* is sad; so is Les Larmes *in* Werther.... But a very great deal of supermusic is neither grand nor sad. Haydn's symphonies are usually as light-hearted and as light-waisted as possible. Mozart's *Figaro* scarcely seems to have a care. Listen to Beethoven's *Fourth* and *Eighth Symphonies*, *Il Barbiere* again, *Die Meistersinger*.... But do not be misled: Massenet's *Don Quichotte* is light music; so is Mascagni's *Lodoletta*....

Is music to be prized and taken to our hearts because it is contrapuntal and complex? We frequently hear it urged that Bach (who was more or less forgotten for a hundred years, by the way) was the greatest of composers and his music is especially intricate. He is the one composer, indeed, who can *never* be played with one finger! But poor unimportant forgotten Max Reger also wrote in the most complicated forms; the great Gluck in the simplest. Gluck, indeed, has even been considered weak in counterpoint and fugue. Meyerbeer, it is said, was also weak in counterpoint and fugue. Is he therefor to be regarded as the peer of Gluck? Is Mozart's *G minor Symphony* more important (because it is more complicated) than the same composer's, *Batti, Batti*?

We learn from some sources that music stands or falls by its melody but what is good melody? According to his contemporaries Wagner's music dramas were lacking in melody. ***Sweet Marie*** is certainly a melody; why is it not as good a melody as ***The Old Folks at Home***? Why is Musetta's waltz more popular than Gretel's? It is no better as melody. As a matter of fact there is, has been, and for ever will be war over this question of melody, because the point of view on the subject is continually changing. As Cyril Scott puts it in his book, "The Philosophy of Modernism": "at one time it (melody) extended over a few bars and then came to a close, being, as it were, a kind of sentence, which, after running for the moment, arrived at a full stop, or semicolon. Take this and compare it with the modern tendency: for that modern tendency is to argue that a melody might go on indefinitely almost; there is no reason why it should come to a full stop, for it is not a sentence, but more a line, which, like the rambling incurvations of a frieze, requires no rule to stop it, but alone the will and taste of its engenderer."

Or is harmonization the important factor? Folk-songs are not harmonized at all, and yet certain musicians, Cecil Sharp for example, devote their lives to collecting them, while others, like Percy Grainger, base their compositions on them. On the other hand such music as Debussy's ***Iberia*** depends for its very existence on its beautiful harmonies. The harmonies of Gluck are extremely simple, those of Richard Strauss extremely complex.

H. T. Finck says somewhere that one of the greatest charms of music is modulation but the old church composers who wrote in the "modes" never modulated at all. Erik Satie seldom avails himself of this modern device. It is a question whether Leo Ornstein modulates. If we may take him at his word Arnold Schoenberg has a system of modulation. At least it is his very own.

Are long compositions better than short ones? This may seem a silly question but I have read criticisms based on a theory that they were.

Listen, for example, to de Quincy: "A song, an air, a tune,--that is,
a short succession of notes revolving rapidly upon itself,--how could
that by possibility offer a field of compass sufficient for the
development of great musical effects? The preparation pregnant with
the future, the remote correspondence, the questions, as it were,
which to a deep musical sense are asked in one passage, and answered
in another; the iteration and ingemination of a given effect, moving
through subtle variations that sometimes disguise the theme,
sometimes fitfully reveal it, sometimes throw it out tumultuously to
the daylight,--these and ten thousand forms of self-conflicting
musical passion--what room could they find, what opening, for
utterance, in so limited a field as an air or song?" After this
broadside permit me to quote a verse of Gerard de Nerval:

> "Il est un air pour qui je donnerais
> Tout Rossini, tout Mozart, et tout Weber,
> Un air tres-vieux, languissant et funebre,
> Qui pour moi seul a des charmes secrets."

And now let us dispassionately, if possible, regard the evidence.
Richard Strauss's **Alpine Symphony**, admittedly one of his weakest
works and considered very tiresome even by ardent Straussians, plays
for nearly an hour while any one can sing **Der Erlkonig** in three
minutes. Are short compositions better than long ones? Answer: Love
me and the World is Mine is a short song (although it seldom sounds
so) while Schubert's **C major Symphony** is called the "symphony of
heavenly length."

Is what is new better than what is old? Is what is old better than
what is new? Schoenberg is new; is he therefor to be considered better
than Beethoven? Stravinsky is new; is he therefor to be considered
worse than Liszt?

Is an opera better than a song? Compare ***Pagliacci*** and Strauss's
Standchen. Is a string quartet better than a piece for the piano?
But I grow weary.... Under the circumstances it would seem that if you
have any strong opinions about music you are perfectly entitled to
them, for the critics do not agree and you will find many of them
basing their criticism on some of the various hypotheses I have
advanced. H. T. Finck tells us that the sonata form is illogical,
forgetting perhaps that once it served its purpose; Jean Marnold
dubbed ***Armide*** an ***oeuvre batarde***; John F. Runciman called
Parsifal "decrepit stuff," while Ernest Newman assures us that it
is "marvellous"; Pierre Lalo and Philip Hale disagree on the subject
of Debussy's ***La Mer*** while W. J. Henderson and James Huneker wrangle
over Richard Strauss's ***Don Quixote***.

The clue to the whole matter lies in a short phrase: Imitative work is
always bad. Music that tries to be something that something else has
been may be thrown aside as worthless. It will not endure although it
may sometimes please the zanies and jackoclocks of a generation. The
critic, therefor, who comes nearest to the heart of the matter, is he
who, either through instinct or familiarity with the various phenomena
of music, is able to judge of a work's originality. There must be
individuality in new music to make it worthy of our attention, and
that, after all is all that matters. For the tiniest folk-song often
persists in the hearts and minds of the people, often stirs the pulse
of a musician, pursuing its tuneful way through two centuries, while a
mighty thundering symphony of the same period may lie dead and
rotting, food for the Niptus Hololencus and the Blatta Germanica. We
still sing ***The Old Folks At Home*** and ***Le Cycle du Vin*** but we have
laid aside ***Di Tanti Palpiti***. Any piece of music possessing the
certain magic power of individuality is of value, it matters not
whether it be symphony or song, opera or dance. What most critics
have forgotten is that in Music matter, form, and idea are one. In
painting, in poetry the idea, the words, the form, may be separated;

each may play its part, but in music there is no idea without form, no form without idea. That is what makes musical criticism difficult.

January 24, 1918.

Edgar Saltus

"O no, we never mention him,
His name is never heard!"

Old Ballad.

Edgar Saltus

To write about Edgar Saltus should be *vieux jeu*. The man is an American; he was born in 1858; he accomplished some of his best work in the Eighties and the Nineties, in the days when mutton-legged sleeves, whatnots, Rogers groups, cat-tails, peacock feathers, Japanese fans, musk-mellon seed collars, and big-wheeled bicycles were in vogue. He has written history, fiction, poetry, literary criticism, and philosophy, and to all these forms he has brought sympathy, erudition, a fresh point of view, and a radiant style. He has imagination and he understands the gentle art of arranging facts in kaleidoscopic patterns so that they may attract and not repel the reader. America, indeed, has not produced a round dozen authors who equal him as a brilliant stylist with a great deal to say. And yet this man, who wrote some of his best books in the Eighties and who is still alive, has been allowed to drift into comparative oblivion. Even his early reviewers shoved him impatiently aside or ignored him altogether; a writer in "Belford's Magazine" for July, 1888, says: "Edgar Saltus should have his name changed to Edgar Assaulted." Soon he became a literary leper. The doctors and professors would have none of him. To most of them, nowadays, I suppose, he is only a name. Many of them have never read any of his books. I do not even remember to have seen him mentioned in the works of James Huneker and you will not find his name in Barrett Wendell's "A History of American Literature" (1901), "A Reader's History of American Literature" by Thomas Wentworth Higginson and Henry Walcott Boynton (1903), Katherine Lee Bates's "American Literature" (1898), "A Manual of American Literature," edited by Theodore Stanton (1909), William B. Cairns's "A History of American Literature" (1912), William Edward Simonds's "A Student's History of American Literature" (1909), Fred Lewis Pattee's "A History of American Literature Since 1870" (1915), John Macy's "The Spirit of American Literature" (1913), or William Lyon Phelps's "The Advance of the English Novel" (1916). The third volume of "The Cambridge History of American Literature," bringing the subject up to 1900, has not yet appeared but I should be amazed to discover that the editors had decided to include Saltus therein. Curiously enough he is mentioned in Oscar Fay Adams's "A Dictionary of American Authors" (1901 edition) and, of all places, I have found a reference to him in one of Agnes Repplier's books.

You will find few essays about the man or his work in current or anterior periodicals. There is, to be sure, the article by Ramsay Colles, entitled "A Publicist: Edgar Saltus," published in the "Westminster Magazine" for October, 1904, but this essay could have won our author no adherents. If any one had the courage to wade through its muddy paragraphs he doubtless emerged vowing never to read

Saltus. Besides only the novels are touched on. In 1903 G. F. Monkshood and George Gamble arranged a compilation from Saltus's work which they entitled "Wit and Wisdom from Edgar Saltus" (Greening and Co., London). The work is done without sense or sensitiveness and the prefatory essay is without salt or flavour of any sort. An anonymous writer in "Current Literature" for July, 1907, asks plaintively why this author has been permitted to remain in obscurity and quotes from some of the reviews. In "The Philistine" for October, 1907, Elbert Hubbard takes a hand in the game. He says, "Edgar Saltus is the best writer in America--with a few insignificant exceptions," but he deplores the fact that Saltus knows nothing about the cows and chickens; only cities and gods seem to interest him. Still there is some atmosphere in this study, which is devoted to one book, "The Lords of the Ghostland." In the New York Public Library four of Saltus's books and one of his translations (about one-sixth of his published work) are listed. You may also find there in a series of volumes entitled "Nations of the World" his supplementary chapters bringing the books up to date. That is all.

All these years, of course, Saltus has had his admiring circle,[1] people of intelligence, of whom, unfortunately, I cannot say that I was one. These, who have been content to read and admire without spreading the news, may well be inclined to regard my performance as repetitive and impertinent. Of these I must crave indulgence and of Saltus himself too. For he, knowing how well he has done his work, must sit like Buddha, ironic and indulgent, smiling on the poor benighted who have yet to approach his altars. Once, at least, he spoke: "A book that pleases no one may be poor. The book that pleases every one is detestable."

I seem to remember to have heard his name all my life, but until recently I have not read one line concerning or by him. I find that my friends, many of whom are extensive readers, are in the same sad state of ignorance. There is an exception and that exception is responsible for my conversion. For six years, no less, Edna Kenton has been urging me to read Edgar Saltus. She has been gently insinuating but firm. None of us can struggle forever against fate or a determined woman. In the end I capitulated, purchased a book by Edgar Saltus at random, and read it ... at one sitting. I sought for more. As most of his books are out of print and as the list in the Public Library conspicuously omits all but one of his best *opera* the matter presented difficulties. However, a little diligent search in the old book shops accomplished wonders. In less than two weeks I had dug up twenty-two titles and in less than two weeks I had read twenty-four; since then I have consumed the other four. There are few writers in American or any other literature who can survive such a test; there are few writers who have given me such keen pleasure.

The events of his life, mostly remain shrouded in mystery. His comings and goings are not reported in the newspapers; he does not make public speeches; and his name is seldom, if ever, mentioned "among those present." That he has been married and has one daughter "Who's Who" proclaims, together with the few biographical details mentioned below. That is all. May we not herein find some small explanation for his apparent neglect? Many thousands of lesser men have lifted themselves to "literary" prominence by blowing their own tubas and striking their own crotals. Even in the case of a man of such manifest genius as George Bernard Shaw we may be permitted to doubt if he would be so well known, had he not taken the trouble to erect monuments to himself on every possible occasion in every possible location. Fame is a quaint old-fashioned body, who loves to be pursued. She seldom, if ever, runs after anybody except in her well-known role of necrophile.

Edgar Evertson Saltus was born in New York City June 8, 1858. He is a lineal descendant of Admiral Kornelis Evertson, the commander of the Dutch fleet, who captured New York from the English, August 9, 1673.

Francis Saltus, the poet, was his brother. He enjoyed a cosmopolitan education which may be regarded as an important factor in the development of his tastes and ideas. From St. Paul's School in Concord he migrated to the Sorbonne in Paris, and thence to Heidelberg and Munich, where he bathed in the newer Germanic philosophies. Finally he took a course of law at Columbia University. The influence of this somewhat heterogeneous seminary life is manifest in all his future writing. Beginning, no doubt, as a disciple of Emerson in New England, he fell under the spell of Balzac in Paris, of Schopenhauer and von Hartmann in Germany. Pages might be brought forward as evidence that he had a thorough classical education. His knowledge of languages made it easy for him to drink deeply at many fountain heads. If Oscar Wilde found his chief inspiration in Huysmans's "A Rebours," it is certain that Saltus also quaffed intoxicating draughts at this source. Indeed in one of his books he refers to Huysmans as his friend. It is further apparent that he is acquainted with the works of Barbey d'Aurevilly, Josephin Peladan,[2] Baudelaire, Mallarme, Verlaine, Arthur Rimbaud, Catulle Mendes, and Jules Laforgue, especially the Laforgue of the "Moralites Legendaires." His kinship with these writers is near, but through this mixed blood run strains inherited from the early pagans, the mediaeval monks, the Germanic philosophers, and London of the Eighteen Nineties (although there is not one word about Saltus in Holbrook Jackson's book of the period), and perhaps, after all, his nearest literary relative was an American, Edgar Allan Poe, who bequeathed to him a garret full of strange odds and ends. But Saltus surpasses Poe in almost every respect save as a poet.

Joseph Hergesheimer has expressed a theory to the effect that great art is always provincial, never cosmopolitan; that only provincial art is universal in its appeal. Like every other theory this one is to a large extent true, but Hergesheimer in his arbitrary summing up, has forgotten the fantastic. The fantastic in literature, in art of any kind, can never be provincial. The work of Poe is not provincial; nor

is that of Gustave Moreau, an artist with whom Edgar Saltus can very
readily be compared. If you have visited the Musee Moreau in Paris
where, in the studio of the dead painter, is gathered together the
most complete collection of his works, which lend themselves to
endless inspection, you can, in a sense, reconstruct for yourself an
idea of the works of Edgar Saltus. One finds therein the same
unicorns, the same fabulous monsters, the same virgins on the rocks,
the same exotic and undreamed of flora and fauna, the same mystic
paganism, the same exquisitely jewelled workmanship. One can find
further analogies in the Aubrey Beardsley of "Under the Hill," in the
elaborate stylized irony of Max Beerbohm. Surely not provincials
these, but just as surely artists.

Moreover Saltus's style may be said to possess American
characteristics. It is dashing and rapid, and as clear as the water in
Southern seas. The man has a penchant for short and nervous sentences,
but they are never jerky. They explode like so many firecrackers and
remind one of the great national holiday!... Nevertheless Edgar Saltus
should have been born in France.

His essays, whether they deal with literary criticism, history,
religion (which is almost an obsession with this writer),
devil-worship, or cooking, are pervaded by that rare quality, charm.
Somewhere he quotes a French aphorism:

> "Etre riche n'est pas l'affaire,
> Toute l'affaire est de charmer,"

which might be applied to his own work. There is a deep and beneficent
guile in the simplicity of his style, as limpid as a brook, and yet,
as over a brook, in its overtones hover a myriad of sparkling
dragon-flies and butterflies; in its depths lie a plethora of trout.
He deals with the most obstruse and abstract subjects with such ease

and grace, without for one moment laying aside the badge of authority, that they assume a mysterious fascination to catch the eye of the passerby. In his fictions he has sometimes cultivated a more hectic style, but that in itself constitutes one of the bases of its richness. Scarcely a word but evokes an image, a strange, bizarre image, often a complication of images. He is never afraid of the colloquial, never afraid of slang even, and he often weaves lovely patterns with obsolete or technical words. These lines, in which Saltus paid tribute to Gautier, he might, with equal justice, have applied to himself: "No one could torment a fancy more delicately than he; he had the gift of adjective; he scented a new one afar like a truffle; and from the Morgue of the dictionary he dragged forgotten beauties. He dowered the language of his day with every tint of dawn and every convulsion of sunset; he invented metaphors that were worth a king's ransom, and figures of speech that deserve the Prix Montyon. Then reviewing his work, he formulated an axiom which will go down with a nimbus through time: Whomsoever a thought however complex, a vision however apocalyptic, surprises without words to convey it, is not a writer. The inexpressible does not exist." It is impossible to taste at this man's table. One must eat the whole dinner to appreciate its opulent inevitability. Still I may offer a few olives, a branch or two of succulent celery to those who have not as yet been invited to sit down. One of his ladies walks the Avenue in a gown the "color of fried smelts." Such figurative phrases as "Her eyes were of that green-grey which is caught in an icicle held over grass," "The sand is as fine as face powder, **nuance** Rachel, packed hard," "Death, it may be, is not merely a law but a place, perhaps a garage which the traveller reaches on a demolished motor, but whence none can proceed until all old scores are paid," "The ocean resembled nothing so much as an immense blue syrup," "She was a pale freckled girl, with hair the shade of Bavarian beer," "The sun rose from the ocean like an indolent girl from her bath," "Night, that queen who reigns only when she falls, shook out the shroud she wears for gown," are to be found on every page. Certain phrases sound good to him and are re-used: "Disappearances are deceptive," "ruedelapaixian" (to describe a dress), "toilet of the ring" (lifted from the bull-fight in "Mr. Incoul's Misadventure" to do service in an account of the arena games under Nero in "Imperial Purple"), but repetition of this kind is infrequent in his works and seemingly unnecessary. Ideas and phrases, endless chains of them, spurt from the point of his ardent pen. Standing on his magic carpet he shakes new sins out of his sleeve as a conjurer shakes out white rabbits and juggles words with an exquisite dexterity. He is, indeed, the ***jongleur de notre ame***!

From the beginning, his style has attracted the attention of the few and no one, I am sure, has ever written a three line review of a book by Saltus without referring to it. Mme. Amelie Rives has quoted Oscar Wilde as saying to her one night at dinner, "In Edgar Saltus's work passion struggles with grammar on every page!" Percival Pollard has dubbed him a "prose paranoiac," and Elbert Hubbard says, "He writes so well that he grows enamoured of his own style and is subdued like the dyer's hand; he becomes intoxicated on the lure of lines and the roll of phrases. He is woozy on words--locoed by syntax and prosody. The libation he pours is flavoured with euphues. It is all like a cherry in a morning Martini." A phrase which Remy de Gourmont uses to describe Villiers de l'Isle Adam might be applied with equal success to the author of "The Lords of the Ghostland": "L'idealisme de Villiers etait un veritable idealisme verbal, c'est-a-dire qu'il croyait vraiment a la puissance evocatrice des mots, a leur vertu magique." And we may listen to Saltus's own testimony in the matter: "It may be noted that in literature only three things count, style, style polished, style repolished; these imagination and the art of transition aid, but do not enhance. As for style, it may be defined as the sorcery of syllables, the fall of sentences, the use of the exact term, the pursuit of a repetition even unto the thirtieth and fortieth line. Grammar is an adjunct but not an obligation. No grammarian ever wrote a thing that was fit to read."

At his worst--and his worst can be monstrous!--garbed fantastically in purple patches and gaudy rags, he wallows in muddy puddles of Burgundy and gold dust; even then he is unflagging and holds the attention in a vise. His women have eyes which are purple pools, their hair is bitten by combs, their lips are scarlet threads. Even the names of his characters, Roanoke Raritan, Ruis Ixar, Tancred Ennever, Erastus Varick, Gulian Verplank, Melancthon Orr, Justine Dunnellen, Roland Mistrial, Giselle Oppensheim, Yoda Jones, Stella Sixmuth, Violet Silverstairs, Sallie Malakoff, Shane Wyvell, Dugald Maule, Eden Menemon (it will be observed that he has a persistent, balefully procacious, perhaps, indeed, Freudian predilection for the letters U, V, and X),[3] are fantastic and fabulous ... sometimes almost frivolous. And here we may find our paradox. His sense of humour is abnormal, sometimes expressed directly by way of epigram or sly wording but may it not also occasionally express itself indirectly in these purple towers of painted velvet words, extravagant fables, and unbelievable characters he is so fond of erecting? Some of his work almost approaches the burlesque in form. He carries his manner to a point where he seems to laugh at it himself, and then, with a touch of poignant realism or a poetic phrase, he confounds the reader's judgment. The virtuosity of the performance is breath-taking!

He is always the snob (somewhere he defends the snob in an essay): rich food ("half-mourning" [artichoke hearts and truffles], "filet of reindeer," a cygnet in its plumage bearing an orchid in its beak, "heron's eggs whipped with wine into an amber foam," "mashed grasshoppers baked in saffron"), rich clothes, rich people interest him. There is no poverty in his books. His creatures do not toil. They cut coupons off bonds. Sometimes they write or paint, but for the most part they are free to devote themselves exclusively to the pursuit of emotional experience, eating, reading, and travelling the while. And when they have finished dining they wipe their hands, wetted in a golden bowl, in the curly hair of a tiny serving boy. A character in "Madam Sapphira" explains this tendency: "A writer, if he happens to be worth his syndicate, never chooses a subject. The subject chooses him. He writes what he must, not what he might. That's the thing the public can't understand."

There is always a preoccupation with ancient life, sometimes freely expressed as in "Imperial Purple," but more often suggested by plot, phrase, or scene. He kills more people than Caligula killed during the whole course of his bloody reign. Murders, suicides, and other forms of sudden death flash their sensations across his pages. Webster and the other Elizabethans never steeped themselves so completely in gore. In almost every book there is an orgy of death and he has been ingenious in varying its forms. The poisons of rafflesia, muscarine, and orsere are introduced in his fictions; somewhere he devotes an essay to toxicology. Daggers with blades like needles, pistols, drownings, asphyxiations, play their roles ... and in one book there is a crucifixion!

Again I find that Mr. Saltus has said his word on the subject: "In fiction as in history it is the shudder that tells. Hugo could find no higher compliment for Baudelaire than to announce that the latter had discovered a new one. For new shudders are as rare as new vices; antiquity has made them all seem trite. The apt commingling of the horrible and the trivial, pathos and ferocity, is yet the one secret of enduring work--a secret, parenthetically, which Hugo knew as no one else."

His fables depend in most instances upon sexual abberrations, curious coincidences, fantastic happenings. Rapes and incests decorate his pages. He does not ask us to believe his monstrous stories; he compels us to. He carries us by means of the careless expenditure of many passages of somewhat ribald beauty, along with him, captive to his pervasive charm. We are constantly reminded, in endless, almost wearisome, imagery, of gold and purple, foreign languages, esoteric philosophies, foods the names of which strike the ear as graciously as they themselves might strike the tongue. From Huysmans he has learned the formula for ravishing all our senses. Words are often used for their own sakes to call up images, colour flits across every page, across, indeed, every line. We taste, we smell, we see. There is the pomp and circumstance of the Roman Catholic ritual in these pages, the Roman Catholic ritual well supplied with mythical monsters, singing flowers, and blooming women. Strange scarlet and mulberry threads form the woof of these tapestries, threads pulled with great labour from all the art of the past. There is, in much of his work, an undercurrent of subtle sensuous erotic poison; in one of her stories Edna Kenton tells us that ***chartreuse jaune*** and bananas form such a poison. There is a suggestion of ***chartreuse jaune*** and bananas in much of the work of Edgar Saltus.

He is constantly obsessed by the mysteries of love and death, the veils of Isis, the secrets of Moses. While others were delving in the American soil his soul sped afar; he is not even a cosmopolitan; he is a Greek, a Brahmin, a worshipper of Ishtar. There is a prodigious and prodigal display of genius in his work, savannahs of epigrams, forests of ideas, phrases enough to fill the ocean.[4] There is enough material in the romances of Edgar Saltus to furnish all the cinema companies in America with scenarios for a twelve-month.

Early in the Eighties a writer in "The Argus" referred to him as "the prose laureate of pessimism." His philosophy may be summed up in a few phrases: Nothing matters, Whatever will be is, Everything is possible, and Since we live today let us make the best of it and live in Paris. And through all the ***opera*** of Saltus, through the rapes and murders, the religious, philosophical, and social discussions, rings

Cherubino's still unanswered question, *Che cosa e amor?* like a
persistent refrain.

After having said so much it seems unnecessary to add that I strongly
advise the reader to go out and buy all the books of Edgar Saltus he
can find (and to find many will require patience and dexterity, as
most of them are out of print). To further aid him in the matter I
have prepared a short catalogue and with his permission I will guide
him gently through this new land. I have also added a list of
publishers, together with the dates of publication, although I cannot,
in some instances, vouch for their having been the original imprints.
It may be noted that almost all his books have been reprinted in
England.[5]

"Balzac,"[6] signed Edgar Evertson Saltus (for a time he used his full
name) is such good literary criticism and such good personal biography
that one wishes the author had tried the form again. He did not save
in his prefaces to his translations, his essay on Victor Hugo, and his
short study of Oscar Wilde. In its miniature way, for the book is
slight, "Balzac" is as good of its kind as James Huneker's "Chopin,"
Auguste Ehrhard's "Fanny Elssler," and Frank Harris's "Oscar Wilde."
In style it is superior to any of these. It is a very pretty
performance for a debut and if it is out of print, as I think it is,
some enterprising publisher should serve it to the public in a new
edition. The two most interesting chapters, largely anecdotal but
continuously illuminating, are entitled "The Vagaries of Genius,"
wherein one may find an infinitude of details concerning the manner
in which Balzac worked, and "The Chase for Gold," but tucked in
somewhere else is a charming digression about realism in fiction and
the bibliography should still be of use to students. Saltus tells us
that Balzac took all his characters' names from life, frequently from
signs which he observed on the street. In this respect Saltus
certainly has not followed him; in another he has been more imitative:

I refer to the Balzacian trick of carrying people from one book to another.

"The Philosophy of Disenchantment"[7] is an ingratiating account of the pessimism of Schopenhauer, a philosophy with which it would seem, Saltus is fully in accord. Two-thirds of the book is allotted to Schopenhauer, but the remainder is devoted to an exposition of the teachings of von Hartmann and a final essay, "Is Life an Affliction?" which query the author seems to answer in the affirmative. One of the best-known of the Saltus books, "The Philosophy of Disenchantment" is written in a clear, translucent style without the iridescence which decorates his later *opera*.

"After-Dinner Stories from Balzac, done into English by Myndart Verelst (obviously E. S.) with an introduction by Edgar Saltus"[8] contains four of the Frenchman's tales, "The Red Inn," "Madame Firmiani," "The 'Grande Breteche'," and "Madame de Beauseant." The introduction is written in Saltus's most beguiling manner and may be referred to as one of the most delightful short essays on Balzac extant. The dedication is to V. A. B.

"The Anatomy of Negation"[9] is Saltus's best book in his earlier manner, which is as free from flamboyancy as early Gothic, and one of his most important contributions to our literature. The work is a history of antitheism from Kapila to Leconte de Lisle and, while the writer in a brief prefatory notice disavows all responsibility for the opinions of others, it can readily be felt that the book is a labour of love and that his sympathy lies with the iconoclasts through the centuries. The chapter entitled, "The Convulsions of the Church," a brief history of Christianity, is one of the most brilliant passages to be found in any of the works of this very brilliant writer. Indeed, if you are searching for the soul of Saltus you could not do better than turn to this chapter. Of Jesus he says, "He was the most

entrancing of nihilists but no innovator." Here is another excerpt:
"Paganism was not dead; it had merely fallen asleep. Isis gave way to
Mary; apotheosis was replaced by canonization; the divinities were
succeeded by saints; and, Africa aiding, the Church surged from
mythology with the Trinity for tiara." Again: "Satan was Jew from horn
to hoof. The registry of his birth is contained in the evolution of
Hebraic thought." Never was any book so full of erudition and ideas so
easy to read, a fascinating *opus*, written by a true sceptic.
Following the Baedeker system, adopted so amusingly by Henry T. Finck
in his "Songs and Song Writers," this book should be triple-starred.

"Tales before Supper, from Theophile Gautier and Prosper Merimee, told
in English by Myndart Verelst and delayed with a proem by Edgar
Saltus."[10] Translation again. The stories are "Avatar" and "The
Venus of Ille." The essay at the beginning is a very charming
performance. This book is dedicated to E. C. R.

"Mr. Incoul's Misadventure,"[11] Saltus's first novel, is also the
best of his numerous fictions. It, too, should be triple-starred in
any guide book through this *opus*-land. In it will be found,
super-distilled, the very essence of all the best qualities of this
writer. It is written with fine reserve; the story holds; the
characters are unusually well observed, felt, and expressed. Irony
shines through the pages and the final cadence includes a murder and a
suicide. For the former, bromide of potassium and gas are utilized in
combination; for the latter laudanum, taken hypodermically, suffices.
There are scenes in Biarritz and Northern Spain which include a
thrilling picture of a bull-fight. There is an interesting glimpse of
the Paris Opera. There is a description of an epithumetic library
which embraces many forbidden titles, (How that "baron of moral
endeavour ... the professional hound of heaven," Anthony Comstock,
would have gloated over these shelves!), a vibrant page about Goya,
and another about a Thibetian cat. Many passages could be brought

forward as evidence that Mr. Saltus loves the fire-side sphynx. The Mr. Incoul of the title gives one a very excellent idea of how inhuman a just man can be. There is not a single slip in the skilful delineation of this monster. The beautiful heroine vaguely shambles into a tapestried background. She is *moyen age* in her appealing weakness. The *jeune premier*, Lenox Leigh, is well drawn and lighted. Time after time the author strikes subtle harmonies which must have delighted Henry James. Why is this book not dedicated to author of "The Turn of the Screw" rather than to "E. A. S."? The pages are permeated with suspense, horror, information, irony, and charm, about evenly distributed, all of which qualities are expressed in the astounding title (astounding after you have read the book). There is a white marriage in this tale, stipulated in the hymeneal bond. In 1877 Tschaikovsky made a similar agreement with the woman he married.

"The Truth About Tristrem Varick"[12] is written with the same restraint which characterizes the style of "Mr. Incoul's Misadventure," a restraint seldom to be encountered in Saltus's later fictions. One of the angles of the plot in which an irate father attempts to suppress a marriage by suggesting incest, bobs up twice again in his stories, for the last time nearly thirty years later in "The Monster." Irony is the keynote of the work, a keynote sounded in the dedication, "To my master, the philosopher of the unconscious, Eduard von Hartmann, this attempt in ornamental disenchantment is dutifully inscribed." The heroine, as frequently happens with Saltus heroines, is veiled with the mysteries of Isis; we do not see the workings of her mind and so we can sympathize with Varick, who pursues her with persistent misunderstanding and arduous devotion through 240 pages. He attributes her aloofness to his father's unfounded charge against his mother and her father. When he learns that she has borne a child he suspects rape and, with a needle-like dagger that leaves no sign, he kills the man he believes to have seduced her. Then he goes to the lady to receive her thanks, only to learn that she loved the man he has killed. Varick gives himself into the hands of the police, confesses, and is delivered to justice, the lady gloating. A strikingly pessimistic tale, only less good than "Mr. Incoul." There is superb writing in these pages, many delightful passages. La Cenerentola *and* Lucrezia Borgia are mentioned in passing. Saltus has (or had) an exuberant fondness for Donizetti and Rossini. Here is a telling bit of art criticism (attributed to a character) descriptive of the Paris Salon: "There was a Manet or two, a Moreau and a dozen excellent landscapes, but the rest represented the apotheosis of mediocrity. The pictures which Gerome, Cabanel, Bouguereau, and the acolytes of these pastry-cooks exposed were stupid and sterile as church doors." This required courage in 1888. One wonders where Kenyon Cox was at the time! Give this book at least two stars.

"Eden"[13] is the third of Saltus's fictions and possibly the poorest of the three. Eden is the name of the heroine whose further name is Menemon. Stuyvesant Square is her original habitat but she migrates to Fifth Avenue. The tide is flowing South again nowadays. Her husband is almost too good, but nevertheless appearances seem against him until he explains that the lady with whom he has been seen in a cab is his daughter by a former marriage, and the young man who seems to have been making love to Eden is his son. Characteristic of Saltus is the use of the Spanish word for nightingale. There are no deaths, no suicides, no murders in these pages: a very eunuch of a book! A motto from Tasso, "***Perdute e tutto il tempo che in amor non si spende***" adorns the title page and the work is dedicated to "E----H Amicissima."

With "The Pace that Kills"[14] Saltus doffs his old coat and dons a new and gaudier garment. Possibly he owed this change in style to the influence of the London movement so interestingly described in Holbrook Jackson's "The Eighteen-Nineties." The book begins with abortion and ends with a drop over a ferry-boat into the icy East

River. There is an averted strangulation of a baby and for the second time in a Saltus *opus* a dying millionaire leaves his fortune to the St. Nicholas Hospital. Was Saltus ballyhooing for this institution? The hero is a modern Don Juan. Alphabet Jones appears occasionally, as he does in many of the other novels. This Balzacian trick obsessed the author for a time. The book is dedicated to John S. Rutherford and bears as a motto on its title page this quotation from Rabusson: *"Pourquoi la mort? Dites, plutot, pourquoi la vie?"*

In "A Transaction in Hearts"[15] the Reverend Christopher Gonfallon falls in love with his wife's sister, Claire. A New England countess, a subsidiary figure, suggests d'Aurevilly. This story originally appeared in "Lippincott's Magazine" and the editor who accepted it was dismissed. A year or so later a new editor published "The Picture of Dorian Gray." Still later Saltus tells me he met Oscar Wilde in London and the Irish poet asked him for news of the new editor. "He's quite well," answered Saltus. Wilde did not seem to be pleased: "When your story appeared the editor was removed; when mine appeared I supposed he would be hanged. Now you tell me he is quite well. It is most disheartening." Saltus then asked Wilde why Dorian Gray was cut by his friends. Wilde turned it over. "I fancy they saw him eating fish with his knife."

"A Transient Guest and other Episodes"[16] contains three short tales besides the title story: "The Grand Duke's Riches," an account of an ingenious robbery at the Brevoort, "A Maid of Athens," and "Fausta," a story of love, revenge, and death in Cuba. If the final cadence of the book is a dagger thrust the prelude is a subtle poison, rafflesia, a Sumatran plant, intended for the hero, Tancred Ennever, but consumed with fatal results by his faithful fox terrier, Zut Alors. The story is arresting and, as frequently happens in Saltus romances, a man finds himself no match for a woman. "A Transient Guest" is dedicated to K. J. M.

The slender volume entitled "Love and Lore"[17] contains a short series of slight essays, interrupted by slighter sonnets, on subjects which, for the most part, Saltus has treated at greater length and with greater effect elsewhere. He makes a whimsical plea for a modern revival of the Court of Love and in "Morality in Fiction" he derides that Puritanism in American letters whose dark scourge H. L. Mencken still pursues with a cat-o'-nine-tails and a hand grenade. He gives us a fanciful set of rules for a novelist which, happily, he has ignored in his own fictions. The most interesting, personal, and charming chapter, although palpably derived from "The Philosophy of Disenchantment," is that entitled "What Pessimism Is Not"; here again we are in the heart of the author's philosophy. Those who like to read books about the Iberian Peninsula can scarcely afford to miss "Fabulous Andalucia," in which an able brief for the race of Othello is presented: "Under the Moors, Cordova surpassed Baghdad. They wrote more poetry than all the other nations put together. It was they who invented rhyme; they wrote everything in it, contracts, challenges, treaties, treatises, diplomatic notes and messages of love. From the earliest khalyf down to Boabdil, the courts of Granada, of Cordova and of Seville were peopled with poets, or, as they were termed, with makers of Ghazels. It was they who gave us the dulcimer, the hautbois and the guitar; it was they who invented the serenade. We are indebted to them for algebra and for the canons of chivalry as well…. It was from them that came the first threads of light which preceded the Renaissance. Throughout mediaeval Europe they were the only people that thought." The book is dedicated to Edgar Fawcett, "perfect poet--perfect friend" and is embellished with a portrait of its author.

"The Story Without a Name"[18] is a translation of "Une Histoire Sans Nom" of Barbey d'Aurevilly, and is preceded by one of Saltus's charming and atmospheric literary essays, the best on d'Aurevilly to

be found in English. When this book first appeared, Mr. Saltus informs
me, a reviewer, "who contrived to be both amusing and complimentary,"
said that Barbey d'Aurevilly was a fictitious person and that this
vile story was Saltus's own vile work!

"Mary Magdalen,"[19] on the whole disappointing, is nevertheless one
of the important Saltus *opera*. The opening chapters, like Oscar
Wilde's *Salome* (published two years later than "Mary Magdalen") owe
much to Flaubert's "Herodias." The dance on the hands is a detail
from Flaubert, a detail which Tissot followed in his painting of
Salome.... From the later chapters it is possible that Paul Heyse
filched an idea. The turning point of his drama, *Maria von Magdala*,
hinges on Judas's love for Mary and his jealousy of Jesus. Saltus
develops exactly this situation. Heyse's play appeared in 1899, eight
years after Saltus's novel. However, Saltus has protested to me that
it is an idea that might have occurred to any one. "I put it in," he
added, "to make the action more nervous." The book begins well with a
description of Herod's court and Rome in Judea, but as a whole it is
unsatisfactory. Once the plot develops Saltus seems to lose interest.
He lazily quotes whole scenes from the Bible (George Moore very
cleverly avoided this pitfall in "The Brook Kerith"). The early
chapters suggest "Imperial Purple," which appeared a year later and
upon which he may well have been at work at this time. There is a
foreshadowing, too, of "The Lords of the Ghostland" in a very amusing
and slightly cynical passage in which Mary as a child listens to
Sephorah the sorceress tell legends and myths of Assyria and Egypt.
Mary interrupts with "Why you mean Moses! You mean Noah!" just as a
child of today, if confronted with the situations in the Greek dramas
would attribute them to Bayard Veiller or Eugene Walter. Saltus is too
much of a scholar to find much novelty in Christianity. But aside from
this passage cynicism is lacking from this book, a quality which makes
another story on the same theme, "Le Procurateur de Judee," one of the
greatest short stories in any language. Mary's sins are quickly passed

over and we come almost immediately to her conversion. Herod Antipas, with his "fan-shaped beard" and vacillating Pilate, quite comparable to a modern politician, are the most human and best-realized characters in a book which should have been greater than it is. "Mary Magdalen" is dedicated to Henry James.

"The facts in the Curious Case of H. Hyrtl, esq."[20] is a slight yarn in the mellow Stevenson manner, with a kindly old gentleman as the messenger of the supernatural who provides the wherewithal for a marriage between an impoverished artist, who is painting Heliogabolus's feast of roses, and his sweet young thing. Quite a departure this from the usual Saltus manner; nevertheless there are two deaths, one by shock, the other in a railway accident. The plot depends on as many impossible entrances and exits as a Palais Royal farce and the reader is asked to believe in many coincidences. The book is dedicated to Lorillard Ronalds who, the author explains in a few French phrases, asked him to write something "de tres pure et de tres chaste, pour une jeunesse, sans doute." He adds that the story is a rewriting of a tale which had appeared twenty years earlier.

"Imperial Purple"[21] marks the high-tide of Saltus's peculiar genius. The emperors of imperial decadent Rome are led by the chains of art behind the chariot wheels of the poet: Julius Caesar, whom Cato called "that woman," Augustus, Tiberius, Caligula, the wicked Agrippina, for whom Agnes Repplier named her cat, Claudius, Nero, Hadrian, Vespasian, down to the incredible Heliogabolus. Saltus, who has given us many vivid details concerning the lives of his predecessors, seemingly falters at this dread name, but only seemingly. More can be found about this extraordinary and perverse emperor in Lombard's "L'Agonie" and in Franz Blei's "The Powder Puff," but, although Saltus is brief, he evokes an atmosphere and a picture in a few short paragraphs. The sheer lyric quality of this book has remained unsurpassed by this author. Indeed it is rare in all literature. Page after page that

Walter Pater, Oscar Wilde, or J. K. Huysmans might have been glad to sign might be set before you. The man writes with invention, with sap, with urge. Our eyes are not clogged with foot-notes and references. It is plain that our author has delved in the "Scriptores Historiae Augustae," that he has read Lampridius, Suetonius, and the others, but he does not strive to make us aware of it. The historical form has at last found a poet to render it supportable. Blood runs across the pages; gore and booty are the principal themes; and yet Beauty struts supreme through the horror. The author's sympathy is his password, a sympathy which he occasionally exposes, for he is not above pinning his heart to his sleeve, as, for example, when he says, "In spite of Augustus's boast, the city was not by any means of marble. It was filled with crooked little streets, with the atrocities of the Tarquins, with houses unsightly and perilous, with the moss and dust of ages; it compared with Alexandria as London compares with Paris; it had a splendour of its own, but a splendour that could be heightened." Here is a picture of squalid Rome: "In the subura, where at night women sat in high chairs, ogling the passer with painted eyes, there was still plenty of brick; tall tenements, soiled linen, the odor of Whitechapel and St. Giles. The streets were noisy with match-pedlars, with vendors of cake and tripe and coke; there were touts there too, altars to unimportant divinities, lying Jews who dealt in old clothes, in obscene pictures and unmentionable wares; at the crossings there were thimbleriggers, clowns and jugglers, who made glass balls appear and disappear surprisingly; there were doorways decorated with curious invitations, gossipy barber shops, where, through the liberality of politicians, the scum of a great city was shaved, curled and painted free; and there were public houses, where vagabond slaves and sexless priests drank the mulled wine of Crete, supped on the flesh of beasts slaughtered in the arena, or watched the Syrian women twist to the click of castanets." The account of the arena under Nero should not be missed, but it is too long to quote here. The book, which we give three stars, is dedicated to Edwin Albert Schroeder. Fortunately, of all Saltus's works, it is the most readily procurable.

"Imperial Purple" has had a curious history. Belford, Clarke and Co., who hid their identity behind the "Morrill, Higgins" imprint, failed shortly after they had issued the book. "Presently," Mr. Saltus writes me, "a Chicago bibliofilou brought it out as the work of some one else and called it 'The Sins of Nero.'" Meanwhile Greening published it in London and finally Mitchell Kennerley reprinted it in New York. In 1911 Macmillan in London brought out "The Amazing Emperor Heliogabolus" by the Reverend John Stuart Hay of Oxford. In the preface to this book I found the following: "I have also the permission of Mr. E. E. Saltus of Harvard University (*sic*) to quote his vivid and beautiful studies on the Roman Empire and her customs. I am also deeply indebted to Mr. Walter Pater, Mr. J. A. Symonds, and Mr. Saltus for many a *tournure de phrase* and picturesque rendering of Tacitus, Suetonious, Lampridius, and the rest." The Reverend Doctor certainly helped himself to "Imperial Purple." Words, sentences, nay whole paragraphs appear without the formality of quotation marks, without any indication, indeed, save these lines in the preface, that they are not part of the Doctor's own imagination, unless one compares them with the style in which the rest of the book is written. "In one instance," Mr. Saltus writes me, "he gave a paragraph of mine as his own. Later on he added, 'as we have already said' and repeated the paragraph. The plural struck me as singular."

"Madam Sapphira"[22] is a vivid study in unchastened womanhood. We see but little of the lady in the 251 pages of this "Fifth Avenue Story"; her character is exposed to us through the experiences of her poor fool husband, who colloquially would be called a simp, by denizens of the Low World a boob. He redeems himself to some extent by sending Madam Sapphira a belated bouquet of cyanide of potassium. On the whole, though characters and phrases in his work might be brought forward to prove the contrary, Mr. Saltus obviously has a low opinion

of women and thinks that men do better without them. The greater part
of the time he appears to agree with Posthumus:

> "Could I find out
> The woman's part in me! For there's no motion
> That tends to vice in man but I affirm
> It is the woman's part; be it lying, note it
> The woman's; flattering, hers; deceiving, hers;
> Lust and rank thoughts, hers, hers; revenges, hers;
> Ambitions, covetings, changes of prides, disdain,
> Nice longings, slanders, mutability,
> All faults that may be named, nay that hell knows,
> Why, hers, in part or all; but rather, all;
> For even to vice
> They are not constant, but are changing still
> One vice of a minute old for one
> Not half so old as that. I'll write against them,
> Detest them, curse them.--Yet 'tis greater skill
> In a true hate, to pray they have their will:
> The very devils cannot plague them better."

"Enthralled, a story of international life setting forth the curious
circumstances concerning Lord Cloden and Oswald Quain":[23] a mad
opus this, an insane phantasmagoria of crime, avarice, and murder.
For the second time in this author's novels incest plays a role. This
time it is real. Quain is indeed the half-brother of the lady who
desires to marry him. He is as vile and virulent a villain as any who
stalks through the pages of Ann Ker, Eliza Bromley, or Mrs. Radcliffe.
A Dr. Jekyll and Mr. Hyde motive is sounded. An ugly man comes back
from London a handsome fellow after visits to a certain doctor who
rearranges the lines of his face. The transformation is effected every
day now (some of our prominent actresses are said to have benefited
by this operation), but in 1894 the mechanism of the trick must have

been appallingly creaky. This story, indeed, borders on the burlesque and has almost as much claim to the title as "The Green Carnation." Was the author laughing at the Eighteen Nineties? The period is subtly evoked in one detail, constantly reiterated in Saltus's early books: ladies and gentlemen when they leave a room "push aside the portieres." Sometimes the "rings jingle." He has in most instances mercifully spared us further descriptions of the interiors of New York houses at this epoch.... At a dinner party one of the guests refers to Howells as the "foremost novelist who is never read." The book is dedicated to "Cherubina, ***dulcissime rerum***." Saltus returned to the central theme of "Enthralled" in a story called "The Impostor," printed in "Ainslee's" for May, 1917.

"When Dreams Come True"[24] again brings us in touch with Tancred Ennever, the stupid hero of "The Transient Guest." In the meantime he has become an almost intolerable prig. It is probable that Saltus meant more by this fable than he has let appear. The roar of the waves on the coast of Lesbos is distinctly audible for a time and the denoument seems to belong to quite another story.... Ennever has turned author. We are informed that he has completed studies on Huysmans and Leconte de Lisle; he is also engaged on a "Historia Amoris." There is an interesting passage relating to the names of great writers. Alphabet Jones assures us that they are always "in two syllables with the accent on the first. Oyez: Homer, Sappho, Horace, Dante, Petrarch, Ronsard, Shakespeare, Hugo, Swinburne ... Balzac, Flaubert, Huysmans, Michelet, Renan." The reader is permitted to add ... "Saltus"!

"Purple and Fine Women"[25] is a misnamed book. It should be called "Philosophic Fables." The first two stories are French in form. Paul Bourget himself is the hero of one of them! In "The Princess of the Sun" we are offered a new and fantastic version of the Coppelia story. "The Dear Departed" finds Saltus in a murderous amorous mood again. In

"The Princess of the Golden Isles" a new poison is introduced, muscarine. Alchemy furnishes the theme for one tale; the protagonist seeks an alcahest, a human victim for his crucible. We are left in doubt as to whether he chooses his wife, who wears a diamond set in one of her teeth, or a gorilla. There are dramas of dual personality and of death. Metaphysics and spiritualism rise dimly out of the charm of this book. There is a duchess who mews like a cat and somewhere we are assured that ***Perche non posso odiarte*** from ***La Sonnnambula*** is the most beautiful aria in the Italian repertory. Here is a true and soul-revealing epigram: "The best way to master a subject of which you are ignorant is to write it up." Certainly not Saltus at his best, this ***opus***, but far from his worst.

"The Perfume of Eros"[26] is frenzied fiction again; amnesia, drunkenness, white slavery, sex, are its mingled themes. There is a pretty picture, recognizable in any smart community, of a witty woman of fashion, and a full-length portrait of a bounder. "The Yellow Fay," Saltus's ***cliche*** for the Demon Rum, was the original title of this "Fifth Avenue Incident." Romance and Realism consort lovingly together in its pages. There is an unforgetable passage descriptive of a young man ridding himself of his mistress. He interrupts his flow of explanation to hand her a card case, which she promptly throws out of the window.

"'That is an agreeable way of getting rid of twelve thousand dollars,' he remarked.

"Yet, however lightly he affected to speak, the action annoyed him. Like all men of large means he was close. It seemed to him beastly to lose such a sum. He got up, went to the window and looked down. He could not see the case and he much wanted to go and look for it. But that for the moment Marie prevented."

"The Pomps of Satan"[27] is replete with grace and graciousness, and full of charm, a quality more valuable to its possessor than juvenility, our author tells us in a chapter concerning the lost elixir of youth. Neither form nor matter assume ponderous shape in this volume, which in the quality of its contents reminds one faintly of Franz Blei's lady's breviary, "The Powder Puff," but Saltus's book is the more ingratiating of the two. Satan's pomps are varied; the author exposes his whims, his ideas, images the past, forecasts the future, deplores the present. There is a chapter on cooking and we learn that Saltus does not care for food prepared in the German style … nor yet in the American. He forbids us champagne: "Champagne is not a wine. It is a beverage, lighter indeed than brandy and soda, but, like cologne, fit only for demi-reps." But he seems untrue to himself in an essay condemning the use of perfumes. His own books are heavily scented. With the rare prescience and clairvoyance of an artist he includes the German Kaiser in a chapter on hyenas (in 1906!); therein stalk the blood-stained shadows of Caligula, Caracalla, Atilla, Tamerlane, Cesare Borgia, Philip II, and Ivan the Terrible. The paragraph is worth quoting: "Power consists in having a million bayonets behind you. Its diffusion is not general. But there are people who possess it. For one, the German Kaiser. Not long since somebody or other diagnosed in him the habitual criminal. We doubt that he is that. But we suspect that, were it not for the press, he would show more of primitive man than he has thus far thought judicious." Has Mme. de Thebes done better? Saltus also foresaw Gertrude Stein. Peering into the future he wrote: "When that day comes the models of literary excellence will not be the long and windy sentences of accredited bores, but ample brevities, such as the 'N' on Napoleon's tomb, in which, in less than a syllable, an epoch, and the glory of it, is resumed." Saltus forsakes his previous choice from Bellini and installs *Tu che a Dio* as his favourite Italian opera air. Here is another flash of self-revealment: "Byzance is rumoured to have been the sewer of every sin, yet such was its beauty that it is the canker of our heart we could not have lived there." Always this turning to the far past, this delving in rosetta stones and palimpsests, this preoccupation with the sights and sins of the ancient gods and kings. A chapter on poisons, another on Gille de Retz, which probably owes something to "La Bas," betray this preference. He playfully suggests that the Academy of Arts and Letters be filled up with young nobodies: "They have, indeed, done nothing yet. But therein is their charm. An academy composed of young people who have done nothing yet would be more alluring than one made up of fossils who are unable to do anything more." Herein are contained enough aphorisms and epigrams to make up a new book of Solomonic wisdom. Hardly as evenly inspired as "Imperial Purple," "The Pomps of Satan" is more dashing and more varied. It is also more tired.

"Vanity Square"[28] in Stella Sixmuth boasts such a "vampire" as even Theda Bara is seldom called upon to portray. Not until the final chapters of this mystery story do we discover that this lady has been poisoning a rich man's wife, with an eye on the rich man's heart and hand. Oraere is this slow and subtle poison which leaves no subsequent trace. She is thwarted but in a subsequent attempt she is successful. Robert Hichens has used this theme in "Bella Donna." There is a suicide by pistol. An exciting story but little else, this book contains fewer references to the gods and the caesars than is usual with Saltus. To compensate there are long discussions about phobias, dual personalities (a girl with six is described) and theories about future existence. Vanity Square, we are told, is bounded by Central Park, Madison Avenue, Seventy-second Street and the Plaza.

It will be remembered that Tancred Ennever was at work on "Historia Amoris"[29] in 1895, which would seem to indicate that Saltus had begun to collect material for it himself at that time. The title is a literal description of the contents of the book: it is a history of love. Such a work might have been made purely anecdotal or scientific, but Saltus's purpose has been at once more serious and more graceful, to show how the love currents flowed through the centuries, to show what effect period life had on love and what effect love had on period life. Beginning with Babylon and passing on through the "Song of Songs" we meet Helen of Troy, Scheherazade (though but briefly), Sappho (to whom an entire chapter is devoted), Cleopatra (whom Heine called "***cette reine entretenue***"), Mary Magdalen, Heloise.... The Courts of Love are described and deductions are drawn as to the effect of the Renaissance on the Gay Science. "Historia Amoris" is concluded by a Schopenhauerian essay on "The Law of Attraction." Cicisbeism is not treated in extenso, as it should be, and I also missed the fragrant name of Sophie Arnould. Readers of "Love and Lore," "The Pomps of Satan," "Imperial Purple," and "The Lords of the Ghostland" will find much of their material adjusted to the purposes of this History of Love, which, nevertheless, no one interested in Saltus can afford to miss.

In "The Lords of the Ghostland, a history of the ideal,"[30] Saltus returns to the theme of "The Anatomy of Negation." The newer work is both more cynical and more charming. It is, of course, a history and a comparison of religions. With Reinach Saltus believes that Christianity owes much to its ancestors. Brahma, Ormuzd, Amon-Ra, Bel-Marduk, Jehovah, Zeus, Jupiter, and many lesser deities parade before us in defile. Prejudice, intolerance, tolerance even are lacking from this book, as they were from "Imperial Purple." "The Lords of the Ghostland" is neither reverent nor irreverent, it is unreverent. Mr. Saltus finds joy in writing about the gods, the joy of a poet, and if his chiefest pleasure is to extol the gods of Greece that is only what might be expected of this truly pagan spirit. Students of comparative theology can learn much from these pages, but they will learn it unwittingly, for the poet supersedes the teacher. Saltus is never professorial. The scientific spirit is never to the fore; no marshalling of dull facts for their own sakes. Nevertheless I suspect that the book contains more absorbing information than any similar volume on the subject. With a fascinating and guileful style this divine devil of an author leads us on to the spot where he can point out to us that the only original feature of Christianity is the crucifixion, and even that is foreshadowed in Hindoo legend, in which Krishna dies, nailed by arrows to a tree. This book should be required reading for the first class in isogogies.

Most of the scenes of "Daughters of the Rich"[31] are laid in Paris. The plot hinges on mistaken identity and the whole is a very ingenious detective story. The book begins rather than ends with a murder, but that is because the tale is told backward. Through lies, deceit, and treachery the woman in the case, one Sallie Malakoff, betrays the hero into marriage with her. When he discovers her perfidy he cheerfully cuts her throat from ear to ear and goes to join the lady from whom he has been estranged. She receives him with open arms and suggests wedding bells. No woman, she asserts, could resist a man who has killed another woman for her sake. This is decidedly a Roman point of view! Some of the action takes place in a house on the Avenue Malakoff, which must have been near the **hotel** of the Princesse de Sagan and the apartment occupied by Miss Mary Garden.... A fat manufacturer's wife confronts the proposal of a mercenary duke with an epic rejoinder: "Pay a man a million dollars to sleep with my daughter! Never!"... Again Saltus demonstrates how completely he is master of the story-telling gift, how surely he possesses the power to compel breathless attention.

"The Monster"[32] is fiction, incredible, insane fiction. The monster is incest, in this instance *inceste manque* because it doesn't come off. On the eve of a runaway marriage Leilah Ogsten is informed by her father that her intended husband is her own brother (he inculpates her mother in the scandal). Leilah disappears and to put barriers between her and the man she loves becomes the bride of another.

Verplank pursues. There are two fabulous duels and a scene in which our hero is mangled by dogs. The stage (for we are always in some extravagant theatre) is frequently set in Paris and the familiar scenes of the capital are in turn exposed to our view. It is all mad, full of purple patches and crimson splotches and yet, once opened, it is impossible to lay the book down until it is completed. From this novel Mr. Saltus fashioned his only play, *The Gates of Life*, which he sent to Charles Frohman and which Mr. Frohman returned. The piece has neither been produced nor published.

Last year (1917) the Brothers of the Book in Chicago published privately an extremely limited edition (474 copies) of a book by Edgar Saltus entitled, "Oscar Wilde: An Idler's Impression," which contains only twenty-six pages, but those twenty-six pages are very beautiful. They evoke a spirit from the dead. Indeed, I doubt if even Saltus has done better than his description of a strange occurrence in a Regent Street Restaurant on a certain night when he was supping with Wilde and Wilde was reading *Salome* to him: "apropos of nothing, or rather with what to me at the time was curious irrelevance, Oscar, while tossing off glass after glass of liquor, spoke of Pheme, a goddess rare even in mythology, who after appearing twice in Homer, flashed through a verse of Hesiod and vanished behind a page of Herodotus. In telling of her, suddenly his eyes lifted, his mouth contracted, a spasm of pain--or was it dread?--had gripped him. A moment only. His face relaxed. It had gone.

"I have since wondered, could he have evoked the goddess then? For Pheme typified what modern occultism terms the impact--the premonition that surges and warns. It was Wilde's fate to die three times--to die in the dock, to die in prison, to die all along the boulevards of Paris. Often since I have wondered could the goddess have been lifting, however slightly, some fringe of the crimson curtain, behind which, in all its horror, his destiny crouched. If so, he braved it.

"I had looked away. I looked again. Before me was a fat pauper, florid and over-dressed, who, in the voice of an immortal, was reading the fantasies of the damned. In his hand was a manuscript, and we were supping on **Salome**."

Edgar Saltus began with Balzac in 1884 and he has reached Oscar Wilde in 1917. His other literary essays, on Gautier and Merimee in "Tales Before Supper," on Barbey d'Aurevilly in "The Story Without a Name," and on Victor Hugo in "The Forum" (June, 1912,) all display the finest qualities of his genius. Pervaded with his rare charm they are clairvoyant and illuminating, more than that arresting. They should be brought together in one volume, especially as they are at present absolutely inaccessible, terrifyingly so, every one of them. And if they are to be thus collected may we not hope for one or two new essays with, say, for subjects, Flaubert and Huysmans?

It is, you may perceive, as an essayist, a historian, an amateur philosopher that Saltus excels, but his fiction should not be underrated on that account. His novels indeed are half essays, just as his essays are half novels. Even the worst of them contains charming pages, delightful and unexpected interruptions. His series of fables suggests a vast **Comedie Inhumaine** but this statement must not be regarded as dispraise: it is merely description. You will find something of the same quality in the work of Edgar Allan Poe, but Saltus has more grace and charm than Poe, if less intensity. After one dip into realism ("Mr. Incoul's Misadventure") Saltus became an incorrigible romantic. All his characters are the inventions of an errant fancy; scarcely one of them suggests a human being, but they are none the less creations of art. This, perhaps, was a daring procedure in an era devoted to the exploitation in fiction of the facts of hearth and home.... After all, however, his way may be the better way. Personally I may say that my passion for realism is on the wane.

In these strange tales we pass through the familiar haunts of metropolitan life, but the creatures are amazingly unfamiliar. They have horns and hoofs, halos and wings, or fins and tails. An esoteric band of fabulous monsters these: harpies and vampires take tea at Sherry's; succubi and incubbi are observed buying opal rings at Tiffany's; fairies, angels, dwarfs, and elves, bearing branches of asphodel, trip lightly down Waverly Place; peris, amshaspahands, aesir, izeds, and goblins sleep at the Brevoort; seraphim and cherubim decorate drawing rooms on Irving Place; griffons, chimeras, and sphynxes take courses in philosophy at Harvard; willis and sylphs sing airs from **Lucia di Lammermoor** and **Le Nozze di Figaro**; naiads and mermaids embark on the Cunard Line; centaurs and amazons drive in the Florentine Cascine; kobolds, gnomes, and trolls stab, shoot, and poison one another; and a satyr meets the martichoras in Gramercy Park. No such pictures of monstrous, diverting, sensuous existence can be found elsewhere save in the paintings of Arnold Bocklin, Franz von Stuck, and above all those of Gustave Moreau. If he had done nothing else Edgar Saltus should be famous for having given New York a mythology of its own!

January 12, 1918.

The New Art of the Singer

"It's the law of life that nothing new can come into the world without pain."

Karen Borneman.

The New Art of the Singer

The art of vocalization is retarding the progress of the modern music drama. That is the simple fact although, doubtless, you are as accustomed as I am to hearing it expressed *a rebours*. How many times have we read that the art of singing is in its decadence, that soon there would not be one artist left fitted to deliver vocal music in public. The Earl of Mount Edgcumbe wrote something of the sort in 1825 for he found the great Catalani but a sorry travesty of his early favourites, Pacchierotti and Banti. I protest against this misconception. Any one who asserts that there are laws which govern singing, physical, scientific laws, must pay court to other ears than mine. I have heard this same man for twenty years shouting in the market place that a piece without action was not a play (usually the drama he referred to had more real action than that which decorates the progress of *Nellie, the Beautiful Cloak Model*), that a composition without melody (meaning something by Richard Wagner, Robert Franz, or even Edvard Grieg) was not music, that verse without rhyme was not poetry. This same type of brilliant mind will go on to aver (forgetting the Scot) that men who wear skirts are not men, (forgetting the Spaniards) that women who smoke cigars are not women, and to settle numberless other matters in so silly a manner that a ten year old, half-witted school boy, after three minutes light thinking, could be depended upon to do better.

The rules for the art of singing, laid down in the Seventeenth and Eighteenth Centuries, have become obsolete. How could it be otherwise?

They were contrived to fit a certain style of composition. We have but the briefest knowledge, indeed, of how people sang before 1700, although records exist praising the performances of Archilei and others. If a different standard for the criticism of vocalization existed before 1600 there is no reason why there should not after 1917. As a matter of fact, maugre much authoritative opinion to the contrary, a different standard does exist. In certain respects the new standard is taken for granted. We do not, for example, expect to hear male sopranos at the opera. The Earl of Mount Edgcumbe admired this artificial form of voice almost to the exclusion of all others. His favourite singer, indeed, Pacchierotti, was a male soprano. But other breaks have been made with tradition, breaks which are not yet taken for granted. When you find that all but one or two of the singers in every opera house in the world are ignoring the rules in some respect or other you may be certain, in spite of the protests of the professors, that the rules are dead. Their excuse has disappeared and they remain only as silly commandments made to fit an old religion. A singer in Handel's day was accustomed to stand in one spot on the stage and sing; nothing else was required of him. He was not asked to walk about or to act; even expression in his singing was limited to pathos. The singers of this period, Nicolini, Senesino, Cuzzoni, Faustina, Caffarelli, Farinelli, Carestini, Gizziello, and Pacchierotti, devoted their study years to preparing their voices for the display of a certain definite kind of florid music. They had nothing else to learn. As a consequence they were expected to be particularly efficient. Porpora, Caffarelli's teacher, is said to have spent six years on his pupil before he sent him forth to be "the greatest singer in the world." Contemporary critics appear to have been highly pleased with the result but there is some excuse for H. T. Finck's impatience, expressed in "Songs and Song Writers": "The favourites of the eighteenth-century Italian audiences were artificial male sopranos, like Farinelli, who was frantically applauded for such circus tricks as beating a trumpeter in holding on to a note, or racing with an orchestra and getting ahead of it; or Caffarelli, who entertained his audiences by singing, ***in one breath***, a chromatic chain of trills up and down two octaves. Caffarelli was a pupil of the famous vocal teacher Porpora, who wrote operas consisting chiefly of monotonous successions of florid arias resembling the music that is now written for flutes and violins." All very well for the day, no doubt, but could Cuzzoni sing Isolde? Could Faustina sing Melisande? And what modern parts would be allotted to the Julian Eltinges of the Eighteenth Century?

When composers began to set dramatic texts to music trouble immediately appeared at the door. For example, the contemporaries of Sophie Arnould, the "creator" of ***Iphigenie en Aulide***, are agreed that she was greater as an actress than she was as a singer. David Garrick, indeed, pronounced her a finer actress than Clairon. From that day to this there has been a continual triangular conflict between critic, composer, and singer, which up to date, it must be admitted, has been won by the academic pundits, for, although the singer has struggled, she has generally bent under the blows of the critical knout, thereby holding the lyric drama more or less in the state it was in a hundred years ago (every critic and almost every composer will tell you that any modern opera can be sung according to the laws of ***bel canto*** and enough singers exist, unfortunately, to justify this assertion) save that the music is not so well sung, according to the old standards, as it was then. No singer has had quite the courage to entirely defy tradition, to refuse to study with a teacher, to embody her own natural ideas in the performance of music, to found a new school ... but there have been many rebells.

The operas of Mozart, Bellini, Donizetti, and Rossini, as a whole, do not demand great histrionic exertion from their interpreters and for a time singers trained in the old Handelian tradition met every requirement of these composers and their audiences. If more action was

demanded than in Handel's day the newer music, in compensation, was
easier to sing. But even early in the Nineteenth Century we observe
that those artists who strove to be actors as well as singers lost
something in vocal facility (really they were pushing on to the new
technique). I need only speak of Ronconi and Mme. Pasta. The lady was
admittedly the greatest lyric artist of her day although it is
recorded that her slips from true intonation were frequent. When she
could no longer command a steady tone the *beaux restes* of her art
and her authoritative style caused Pauline Viardot, who was hearing
her then for the first time, to burst into tears. Ronconi's voice,
according to Chorley, barely exceeded an octave; it was weak and
habitually out of tune. This baritone was not gifted with vocal
agility and he was monotonous in his use of ornament. Nevertheless
this same Chorley admits that Ronconi afforded him more pleasure in
the theatre than almost any other singer he ever heard! If this critic
did not rise to the occasion here and point the way to the future in
another place he had a faint glimmering of the coming revolution:
"There might, there *should* be yet, a new *Medea* as an opera.
Nothing can be grander, more antique, more Greek, than Cherubini's
setting of the 'grand fiendish part' (to quote the words of Mrs.
Siddons on Lady Macbeth). But, as music, it becomes simply impossible
to be executed, so frightful is the strain on the energies of her who
is to present the heroine. Compared with this character, Beethoven's
Leonora, Weber's Euryanthe, are only so much child's play." This is
topsy-turvy reasoning, of course, but at the same time it is
suggestive.

The modern orchestra dug a deeper breach between the two schools.
Wagner called upon the singer to express powerful emotion, passionate
feeling, over a great body of sound, nay, in many instances, *against*
a great body of sound. (It is significant that Wagner himself admitted
that it was a singer [Madame Schroeder-Devrient] who revealed to him
the possibilities of dramatic singing. He boasted that he was the only

one to learn the lesson. "She was the first artist," writes H. T.
Finck, "who fully revealed the fact that in a dramatic opera there may
be situations where *characteristic* singing is of more importance
than *beautiful* singing.") It is small occasion for wonder that
singers began to bark. Indeed they nearly expired under the strain of
trying successfully to mingle Porpora and passion. According to W. F.
Apthorp, Max Alvary once said that, considering the emotional
intensity of music and situations, the constant co-operation of the
surging orchestra, and, most of all, the unconquerable feeling of the
reality of it all, it was a wonder that singing actors did not go
stark mad, before the very faces of the audience, in parts like
Tristan or Siegfried.... The critics, however, were inexorable; they
stood by their guns. There was but one way to sing the new music and
that was the way of Bernacchi and Pistocchi. In time, by dint of
persevering, talking night and day, writing day and night, they
convinced the singer. The music drama developed but the singer was
held in his place. Some artists, great geniuses, of course, made the
compromise successfully.... Jean de Reszke, for example, and Lilli
Lehmann, who said to H. E. Krehbiel ("Chapters of Opera"): "It is
easier to sing all three Brunnhildes than one Norma. You are so
carried away by the dramatic emotion, the action, and the scene, that
you do not have to think how to sing the words. That comes of itself"
... but they made the further progress of the composer more difficult
thereby; music remained merely pretty. The successors of these supple
singers even learned to sing Richard Strauss with broad cantilena
effects. As for Puccini! At a performance of *Madama Butterfly* a
Japanese once asked why the singers were producing those nice round
tones in moments of passion; why not ugly sounds?

Will any composer arise with the courage to write an opera which
cannot be sung? Stravinsky almost did this in *The Nightingale* but
the break must be more complete. Think of the range of sounds made by
the Japanese, the gipsy, the Chinese, the Spanish folk-singers. The

newest composer may ask for shrieks, squeaks, groans, screams, a thousand delicate shades of guttural and falsetto vocal tones from his interpreters. Why should the gamut of expression on our opera stage be so much more limited than it is in our music halls? Why should the Hottentots be able to make so many delightful noises that we are incapable of producing? Composers up to date have taken into account a singer's apparent inability to bridge difficult intervals. It is only by ignoring all such limitations that the new music will definitely emerge, the new art of the singer be born. What marvellous effects might be achieved by skipping from octave to octave in the human voice! When will the obfusc pundits stop shouting for what Avery Hopwood calls "ascending and descending tetrarchs!"

But, some one will argue, with the passing of **bel canto** what will become of the operas of Mozart, Bellini, Rossini, and Donizetti? Who will sing them? Fear not, lover of the golden age of song, **bel canto** is not passing as swiftly as that. Singers will continue to be born into this world who are able to cope with the floridity of this music, for they are born, not made. Amelita Galli-Curci will have her successors, just as Adelina Patti had hers. Singers of this kind begin to sing naturally in their infancy and they continue to sing, just sing.... One touch of drama or emotion and their voices disappear. Remember Nellie Melba's sad experience with **Siegfried**. The great Mario had scarcely studied singing (one authority says that he had taken a few lessons of Meyerbeer!) when he made his debut in Robert, le Diable and there is no evidence that he studied very much afterwards. Melba, herself, spent less than a year with Mme. Marchesi in preparation for her opera career. Mme. Galli-Curci asserts that she has had very little to do with professors and I do not think Mme. Tetrazzini passed her youth in mastering **vocalizzi**. As a matter of fact she studied singing only six months. Adelina Patti told Dr. Hanslick that she had sung **Una voce poco fa** at the age of seven with the same embellishments which she used later when she appeared in the opera in which the air occurs. No, these singers are freaks of nature like tortoise-shell cats and like those rare felines they are usually females of late, although such singers as Battistini and Bonci remind us that men once sang with as much agility as women. But when this type of singer finally becomes extinct naturally the operas which depend on it will disappear too for the same reason that the works of Monteverde and Handel have dropped out of the repertory, that the Greek tragedies and the Elizabethan interludes are no longer current on our stage. None of our actors understands the style of Chinese plays; consequently it would be impossible to present one of them in our theatre. As Deirdre says in Synge's great play, "It's a heartbreak to the wise that it's for a short space we have the same things only." We cannot, indeed, have everything. No one doubts that the plays of AEschylus, Euripides, and Sophocles are great dramas; the operas I have just referred to can also be admired in the closet and probably they will be. Even today no more than two works of Rossini, the most popular composer of the early Nineteenth Century, are to be heard. What has become of **Semiramide**, **La Cenerentola**, and the others? There are no singers to sing them and so they have been dropped from the repertory without being missed. Can any of our young misses hum **Di Tanti Palpiti**? You know they cannot. I doubt if you can find two girls in New York (and I mean girls with a musical education) who can tell you in what opera the air belongs and yet in the early Twenties this tune was as popular as **Un Bel Di** is today.

Coloratura singing has been called heartless, not altogether without reason. At one time its exemplars fired composers to their best efforts. That day has passed. That day passed seventy years ago. It may occur to you that there is something wrong when singers of a certain type can only find the proper means to exploit their voices in works of the past, operas which are dead. It is to be noted that Nellie Melba and Amelita Galli-Curci are absolutely unfitted to sing in music dramas even so early as those of Richard Wagner; Dukas,

Strauss, and Stravinsky are utterly beyond them. Even Adelina Patti
and Marcella Sembrich appeared in few, if any, new works of
importance. They had no bearing on the march of musical history. Here
is an entirely paradoxical situation; a set of interpreters who exist,
it would seem, only for the purpose of delivering to us the art of the
past. What would we think of an actor who could make no effect save in
the tragedies of Corneille? It is such as these who have kept Leo
Ornstein from writing an opera. Berlioz forewarned us in his
"Memoirs." He was one of the first to foresee the coming day: "We
shall always find a fair number of female singers, popular from their
brilliant singing of brilliant trifles, and odious to the great
masters because utterly incapable of properly interpreting them. They
have voices, a certain knowledge of music, and flexible throats: they
are lacking in soul, brain, and heart. Such women are regular monsters
and all the more formidable to composers because they are often
charming monsters. This explains the weakness of certain masters in
writing falsely sentimental parts, which attract the public by their
brilliancy. It also explains the number of degenerate works, the
gradual degradation of style, the destruction of all sense of
expression, the neglect of dramatic properties, the contempt for the
true, the grand, and the beautiful, and the cynicism and decrepitude
of art in certain countries."

So, even if, as the ponderous criticasters are continually pointing
out, the age of **bel canto** is really passing there is no actual
occasion for grief. All fashions in art pass and what is known as bel
canto is just as much a fashion as the bombastic style of acting that
prevailed in Victor Hugo's day or the "realistic" style of acting we
prefer today. All interpretative art is based primarily on the
material with which it deals and with contemporary public taste. This
kind of singing is a direct derivative of a certain school of opera
and as that school of opera is fading more expressive methods of
singing are coming to the fore. The very first principle of bel

canto, an equalized scale, is a false one. With an equalized scale a singer can produce a perfectly ordered series of notes, a charming string of matched pearls, but nothing else. It is worthy of note that it is impossible to sing Spanish or negro folk-songs with an equalized scale. Almost all folk-music, indeed, exacts a vocal method of its interpreter quite distinct from that of the art song.

We know now that true beauty lies deeper than in the emission of "perfect tone." Beauty is truth and expressiveness. The new art of the singer should develop to the highest degree the significance of the text. Calve once said that she did not become a real artist until she forgot that she had a beautiful voice and thought only of the proper expression the music demanded.

Of the old method of singing only one quality will persist in the late Twentieth Century (mind you, this is deliberate prophecy but it is about as safe as it would be to predict that Sarah Bernhardt will live to give several hundred more performances of **La Dame aux Camelias**) and that is style. The performance of any work demands a knowledge of and a feeling for its style but style is about the last thing a singer ever studies. When, however, you find a singer who understands style, there you have an artist!

Style is the quality which endures long after the singer has lost the power to produce a pure tone or to contrive accurate phrasing and so makes it possible for artists to hold their places on the stage long after their voices have become partially defective or, indeed, have actually departed. It is knowledge of style that accounts for the long careers of Marcella Sembrich and Lilli Lehmann or of Yvette Guilbert and Maggie Cline for that matter. It is knowledge of style that makes De Wolf Hopper a great artist in his interpretation of the music of Sullivan and the words of Gilbert. Some artists, indeed, with barely a shred of voice, have managed to maintain their positions on the stage

for many years through a knowledge of style. I might mention Victor
Maurel, Max Heinrich (not on the opera stage, of course), Antonio
Scotti, and Maurice Renaud.

A singer may be born with the ability to produce pure tones (I doubt
if Mme. Melba learned much about tone production from her teachers),
she may even phrase naturally, although this is more doubtful, but the
acquirement of style is a long and tedious process and one which
generally requires specialization. For style is elusive. An auditor, a
critic, will recognize it at once but very few can tell of what it
consists. Nevertheless it is fairly obvious to the casual listener
that Olive Fremstad is more at home in the music dramas of Gluck and
Wagner than she is in *Carmen* and *Tosca*, and that Marcella Sembrich
is happier when she is singing Zerlina (as a Mozart singer she has had
no equal in the past three decades) than when she is singing *Lakme*.
Mme. Melba sings *Lucia* in excellent style but she probably could not
convince us that she knows how to sing a Brahms song. So far as I know
she has never tried to do so. A recent example comes to mind in Maria
Marco, the Spanish soprano, who sings music of her own country in her
own language with absolutely irresistible effect, but on one occasion
when she attempted *Vissi d'Arte* she was transformed immediately into
a second-rate Italian singer. Even her gestures, ordinarily fully of
grace and meaning, had become conventionalized.

If this quality of style (which after all means an understanding of
both the surface manner and underlying purpose of a composition and an
ability to transmit this understanding across the footlights) is of
such manifest importance in the field of art music it is doubly so in
the field of popular or folk-music. A foreigner had best think twice
before attempting to sing a Swedish song, a Hungarian song, or a
Polish song, popular or folk. (According to no less an authority than
Cecil J. Sharp, the peasants themselves differentiate between the two
and devote to each a *special vocal method*. Here are his words

["English Folk-Song"]: "But, it must be remembered that the vocal method of the folk-singer is inseparable from the folk-song. It is a cult which has grown up side by side with the folk-song, and is, no doubt, part and parcel of the same tradition. When, for instance, an old singing man sings a modern popular song, he will sing it in quite another way. The tone of his voice will change and he will slur his intervals, after the approved manner of the street-singer. Indeed, it is usually quite possible to detect a genuine folk-song simply by paying attention to the way in which it is sung.") Strangers as a rule do not attempt such matters although we have before us at the present time the very interesting case of Ratan Devi. It is a question, however, if Ratan Devi would be so much admired if her songs or their traditional manner of performance were more familiar to us.

On our music hall stage there are not more than ten singers who understand how to sing American popular songs (and these, as I have said elsewhere at some length,[33] constitute America's best claim in the art of music). It is very difficult to sing them well. Tone and phrasing have nothing to do with the matter; it is all a question of style (leaving aside for the moment the important matter of personality which enters into an accounting for any artist's popularity or standing). Elsie Janis, a very clever mimic, a delightful dancer, and perhaps the most deservedly popular artist on our music hall stage, is not a good interpreter of popular songs. She cannot be compared in this respect with Bert Williams, Blanche Ring, Stella Mayhew, Al Jolson, May Irwin, Ethel Levey, Nora Bayes, Fannie Brice, or Marie Cahill. I have named nearly all the good ones. The spirit, the very conscious liberties taken with the text (the vaudeville singer must elaborate his own syncopations as the singer of early opera embroidered on the score of the composer) are not matters that just happen. They require any amount of work and experience with audiences. None of the singers I have named is a novice. Nor will you find novices who are able to sing Schumann and Franz *lieder*, although they may be blessed with well-nigh perfect vocal organs.

Still the music critics with strange persistence continue to adjudge a singer by the old formulae and standards: has she an equalized scale? Has she taste in ornament? Does she overdo the use of **portamento**, **messa di voce**, and such devices? How is her shake? etc., etc. But how false, how ridiculous, this is! Fancy the result if new writers and composers were criticized by the old laws (so they are, my son, but not for long)! Creative artists always smash the old tablets of commandments and it does not seem to me that interpretative artists need be more unprogressive. Acting changes. Judged by the standards by which Edwin Booth was assessed John Drew is not an actor. But we know now that it is a different kind of acting. Acting has been flamboyant, extravagant, and intensely emotional, something quite different from real life. The present craze for counterfeiting the semblance of ordinary existence on the stage will also die out for the stage is not life and representing life on the stage (except in a conventionalized or decorative form) is not art. Our new actors (with our new playwrights) will develop a new and fantastic mode of expression which will supersede the present fashion.... Rubinstein certainly did not play the piano like Chopin. Presently a **virtuoso** will appear who will refuse to play the piano at all and a new instrument without a tempered scale will be invented so that he may indulge in all the subtleties between half-tones which are denied to the pianist.

It's all very well to cry, "Halt!" and "Who goes there?" but you can't stop progress any more than you can stop the passing of time. The old technique of the singer breaks down before the new technique of the composer and the musician with daring will go still further if the singer will but follow. Would that some singer would have the complete courage to lead! But do not misunderstand me. The road to Parnassus is no shorter because it has been newly paved. Indeed I think it is longer. Caffarelli studied six years before he made his debut as "the greatest singer in the world" but I imagine that Waslav Nijinsky studied ten before he set foot on the stage. The new music drama, combining as it does principles from all the arts is all-demanding of its interpreters. The new singer must learn how to move gracefully and awkwardly, how to make both fantastic and realistic gestures, always unconventional gestures, because conventions stamp the imitator. She must peer into every period, glance at every nation. Every nerve centre must be prepared to express any adumbration of plasticity. Many of the new operas, *Carmen*, *La Dolores*, *Salome*, *Elektra*, to name a few, call for interpretative dancing of the first order. *Madama Butterfly* and *Lakme* demand a knowledge of national characteristics. *Pelleas et Melisande* and *Ariane et Barbe-Bleue* require of the interpreter absolutely distinct enunciation. In Handel's operas the phrases were repeated so many times that the singer was excused if he proclaimed the meaning of the line once. After that he could alter the vowels and consonants to suit his vocal convenience. *Monna Vanna* and *Tristan und Isolde* exact of their interpreters acting of the highest poetic and imaginative scope....

It is a question whether certain singers of our day have not solved these problems with greater success than that for which they are given credit.... Yvette Guilbert has announced publicly that she never had a teacher, that she would not trust her voice to a teacher. The enchanting Yvette practises a sound by herself until she is able to make it; she repeats a phrase until she can deliver it without an interrupting breath, and is there a singer on the stage more expressive than Yvette Guilbert? She sings a little tenor, a little baritone, and a little bass. She can succeed almost invariably in making the effect she sets out to make. And Yvette Guilbert is the answer to the statement often made that unorthodox methods of singing ruin the voice. Ruin it for performances of *Linda di Chaminoux* and *La Sonnambula* very possibly, but if young singers sit about saving their voices for performances of these operas they are more than

likely to die unheard. It is a fact that good singing in the
old-fashioned sense will help nobody out in *Elektra*, Ariane et
Barbe-Bleue, Pelleas et Melisande, *or* The Nightingale. These
works are written in new styles and they demand a new technique. Put
Mme. Melba, Mme. Destinn, Mme. Sembrich, or Mme. Galli-Curci to work
on these scores and you will simply have a sad mess.

We have, I think, but a faint glimmering of what vocal expressiveness
may become. Such torch-bearers as Mariette Mazarin and Feodor
Chaliapine have been procaciously excoriated by the critics. Until
recently Mary Garden, who of all artists on the lyric stage, is the
most nearly in touch with the singing of the future, has been treated
as a charlatan and a fraud. W. J. Henderson once called her the "Queen
of Unsong." Well, perhaps she is, but she is certainly better able to
cope artistically with the problems of the modern music drama than
such Queens of Song as Marcella Sembrich and Adelina Patti would be.
Perhaps Unsong is the name of the new art.

I do not think I have ever been backward in expressing my appreciation
of this artist. My essay devoted to her in "Interpreters and
Interpretations" will certainly testify eloquently as to my previous
attitude in regard to her. But it has not always been so with some of
my colleagues. Since she has been away from us they have learned
something; they have watched and listened to others and so when Mary
Garden came back to New York in *Monna Vanna* in January, 1918, they
were ready to sing choruses of praise in her honour. They have been
encomiastic even in regard to her voice and her manner of singing.

Even my own opinion of this artist's work has undergone a change. I
have always regarded her as one of the few great interpreters, but in
the light of recent experience I now feel assured that she is the
greatest artist on the contemporary lyric stage. It is not, I would
insist, Mary Garden that has changed so much as we ourselves. She has,

it is true, polished her interpretations until they seem incredibly perfect, but has there ever been a time when she gave anything but perfect impersonations of Melisande or Thais? Has she ever been careless before the public? I doubt it.

The fact of the matter is that when Mary Garden first came to New York only a few of us were ready to receive her at anywhere near her true worth. In a field where mediocrity and brainlessness, lack of theatrical instinct and vocal insipidity are fairly the rule her dominant personality, her unerring search for novelty of expression, the very completeness of her dramatic and vocal pictures, annoyed the philistines, the professors, and the academicians. They had been accustomed to taking their opera quietly with their after-dinner coffee and, on the whole, they preferred it that way.

But the main obstacle in the way of her complete success lay in the matter of her voice, of her singing. Of the quality of any voice there can always exist a thousand different opinions. To me the great beauty of the middle register of Mary Garden's voice has always been apparent. But what was not so evident at first was the absolute fitness of this voice and her method of using it for the dramatic style of the artist and for the artistic demands of the works in which she appeared. Thoroughly musical, Miss Garden has often puzzled her critical hearers by singing **Faust** in one vocal style and **Thais** in another. But she was right and they were wrong. She might, indeed, have experimented still further with a new vocal technique if she had been given any encouragement but encouragement is seldom offered to any innovator. As Edgar Saltus puts it, "The number of people who regard a new idea or a fresh theory as a personal insult is curiously large; indeed they are more frequent today than when Socrates quaffed the hemlock." It must, therefore, be a source of ironic amusement to her to find herself now appreciated not alone by her public, which has always been loyal and adoring, but also by the professors themselves.

It would do no harm to any singer to study the multitude of vocal effects this artist achieves. I can think of nobody who could not learn something from her. How, for example, she gives her voice the hue and colour of a *jeune fille* in *Pelleas et Melisande*, for although Melisande had been the bride of Barbe-Bleue before Golaud discovered her in the forest she had never learned to be anything else than innocent and distraught, unhappy and mysterious. Her treatment of certain important phrases in this work is so electrifying in its effect that the heart of every auditor is pierced. Remember, for example, her question to Pelleas at the end of the first act, "*Pourquoi partez-vous?*" to which she imparts a kind of dreamy intuitive longing; recall the amazement shining through her grief at Golaud's command that she ask Pelleas to accompany her on her search for the lost ring: "Pelleas!--Avec Pelleas!--Mais Pelleas ne voudra pas..."; and do not forget the terrified cry which signals the discovery of the hidden Golaud in the park, "Il y a quelqu'un derriere nous!"

In *Monna Vanna* her most magnificent vocal gesture rested on the single word *Si* in reply to Guido's "*Tu ne reviendras pas?*" Her performance of this work, however, offers many examples of just such instinctive intonations. One more, I must mention, her answer to Guido's insistent, "*Cet homme t'a-t-il prise*?"... "J'ai dit la verite.... Il ne m'a pas touchee," sung with dignity, with force, with womanliness, and yet with growing impatience and a touch of sadness.

Let me quote Pitts Sanborn: "It is easy to be flippant about Miss Garden's singing. Her faults of voice and technique are patent to a child, though he might not name them. One who has become a man can ponder the greatness of her singing. I do not mean exclusively in

Debussy, though we all know that as a singer of Debussy ... she has scarce a rival. Take her *mezza voce* and her phrasing in the second act of *Monna Vanna*, take them and bow down before them. Ponder a moment her singing in *Thais*. The converted Thais, about to betake herself desertward with the insistent monk, has a solo to sing. The solo is Massenet, simon-pure Massenet, the idol of the Paris *midinette*. Miss Garden, with a defective voice, a defective technique, exalts and magnifies that passage till it might be the noblest air of Handel or of Mozart. By a sheer and unashamed reliance on her command of style, Miss Garden works that miracle, transfigures Massenet into something superearthly, overpowering. Will you rise up to deny that is singing?"

As for her acting, there can scarcely be two opinions about that! She is one of the few possessors of that rare gift of imparting atmosphere and mood to a characterization. Some exceptional actors and singers accomplish this feat occasionally. Mary Garden has scarcely ever failed to do so. The moment Melisande is disclosed to our view, for example, she seems to be surrounded by an aura entirely distinct from the aura which surrounds Monna Vanna, Jean, Thais, Salome, or Sapho. She becomes, indeed, so much a part of the character she assumes that the spectator finds great difficulty in dissociating her from that character, and I have found those who, having seen Mary Garden in only one part, were quite ready to generalize about her own personality from the impression they had received.

One of the tests of great acting is whether or not an artist remains in the picture when she is not singing or speaking. Mary Garden knows how to listen on the stage. She does not need to move or speak to make herself a part of the action and she is never guilty of such an offence against artistry as that committed by Tamagno, who, according to Victor Maurel, allowed a scene in *Otello* to drop to nothing while he prepared himself to emit a high B.

Watching her magnificent performance of Monna Vanna it struck me that she would make an incomparable Isolde. At the present moment I cannot imagine Mary Garden learning Boche or singing in it even if she knew it, but if some one will present us Wagner's (who hated the Germans as much as Theodore Roosevelt does) music drama in French or English with Mary Garden as Isolde, I think the public will thank me for having suggested it.

Or it would be even better if Schoenberg, or Stravinsky, or Leo Ornstein, inspired by the new light the example of such a singer has cast over our lyric stage, would write a music drama, ignoring the technique and the conventions of the past, as Debussy did when he wrote **Pelleas et Melisande** (creating opportunities which any opera-goer of the last decade knows how gloriously Miss Garden realized). It is thus that the new order will gradually become established. And then the new art ... the new art of the singer....

April 18, 1918.

Au Bal Musette

"Aupres de ma blonde
Qu'il fait bon, fait bon, bon, bon...."

Old French Song.

Au Bal Musette

It has often been remarked by philosophers and philistines alike that the commonest facts of existence escape our attention until they are impressed upon it in some unusual way. For example I knew nothing of the sovereign powers of citronella as a mosquito dispatcher until a plague of the insects drove me to make enquiries of a chemist. For years I believed that knocking the necks off bottles, lacking an opener, was the only alternative. A friend who caught me in this predicament showed me the other use to which the handles of high-boy drawers could be put. It was long my habit to quickly dispose of trousers which had been disfigured by cigarette burns, but that was before I had heard of *stoppage*, a process by which the original weave is cleverly counterfeited. And, wishing to dance, in Paris, I have been guilty of visits to the great dance halls and to the small smart places where champagne is oppressively the only listed beverage. But that was before I discovered the *bal musette*.

One July night in Paris I had dinner with a certain lady at the Cou-Cou, followed by cognac at the Savoyarde. I find nothing strange in this program; it seems to me that I must have dined at the Cou-Cou with every one I have known in Paris from time to time, a range of acquaintanceship including Fernand, the *apache*, and the Comtesse de J----, and cognac at the Savoyarde usually followed the dinner. This evening at the Cou-Cou then resembled any other evening. Do you know how to go there? You must take a taxi-cab to the foot of the hill of Montmartre and then be drawn up in the *finiculaire* to the top where the church of Sacre-Coeur squats proudly, for all the world like a mammoth Buddha (of course you may ride all the way up the mountain in your taxi if you like). From Sacre-Coeur one turns to the left around the board fence which, it would seem, will always hedge in this unfinished monument of pious Catholics; still turning to the left, through the Place du Tertre, in which one must not be stayed by the pleasant sight of the **Montmartroises bourgeoises** eating petite marmite in the open air, one arrives at the Place du Calvaire. The tables of the Restaurant Cou-Cou occupy nearly the whole of this tiny square, to which there are only two means of approach, one up the stairs from the city below, and the other from the Place du Tertre. An artist's house disturbs the view on the side towards Paris; opposite is the restaurant, flanked on the right by a row of modest apartment houses, to which one gains entrance through a high wall by means of a small gate. Sundry visitors to these houses, some on bicycles, make occasional interruptions in the dinner.... From over this wall, too, comes the huge Cheshire cat (much bigger than Alice's, a beautiful animal), which lounges about in the hope, frequently realized, that some one will give him a chicken bone.... Conterminous to the restaurant, on the right, is a tiny cottage, fronted by a still tinier garden, fenced in and gated. Many of the visitors to the Cou-Cou hang their hats and sticks on this fence and its gate. I have never seen the occupants of the cottage in any of my numerous visits to this open air restaurant, but once, towards eleven o'clock the crowd in the square becoming too noisy, the upper windows were suddenly thrown up and a pailful of water descended.... "**Per Baccho!**" quoth the inn-keeper for, it must be known, the Restaurant Cou-Cou is Italian by nature of its **patron** and its cooking.

This night, I say, had been as the others. The Cou-Cou is (and in this respect it is not exceptional in Paris) safe to return to if you have found it to your liking in years gone by. Perhaps some day the small boy of the place will be grown up. He is a real **enfant terrible**. It is his pleasure to **tutoyer** the guests, to amuse himself by pretending to serve them, only to bring the wrong dishes, or none at all. If you call to him he is deaf. Any hope of **revanche** is abandoned in the reflection of the super-retaliations he himself conceives. One young man who expresses himself freely on the subject of Pietro receives a plate of hot soup down the back of his neck, followed immediately by a "***Pardon, Monsieur***," said not without respect. But where might Pietro's father be? He is in the kitchen cooking and if you find your dinner coming too slowly at the hands of the distracted maid servants, who also have to put up with Pietro, go into the kitchen, passing under the little vine-clad porch wherein you may discover a pair of lovers, and help yourself. And if you find some one else's dinner more to your liking than your own take that off the stove instead. At the Cou-Cou you pay for what you eat, not for what you order. And the Signora, Pietro's mother? That unhappy woman usually stands in front of the door, where she interferes with the passage of the girls going for food. She wrings her hands and moans, "***Mon Dieu, quel monde!***" with the idea that she is helping vastly in the manipulation of the machinery of the place.

And the *monde*; who goes there? It is not too *chic*, this *monde*, and yet it is surely not *bourgeois*; if one does not recognize M. Rodin or M. Georges Feydeau, yet there are compensations.... The girls who come attended by bearded companions, are unusually pretty; one sees them afterwards at the bars and *bals* if one does not go to the Abbaye or Pages.... It makes a very pleasant picture, the Place du Calvaire towards nine o'clock on a summer night when tiny lights with pink globes are placed on the tables. The little square twinkles with them and the couples at the tables become very gay, and sometimes sentimental. And when the pink lights appear a small boy in blue trousers comes along to light the street lamp. Then the urchins gather on the wall which hedges in the garden on the fourth side of the square and chatter, chatter, chatter, about all the things that French boys chatter about. Naturally they have a good deal to say about the people who are eating.

I have described the Cou-Cou as it was this night and as it has been all the nights during the past eight summers that I have been there. The dinner too is always the same. It is served *a la carte*, but one is not given much choice. There is always a *potage*, always *spaghetti*, always chicken and a salad, always a lobster, and *zabaglione* if one wants it. The wine--it is called *chianti*--is tolerable. And the *addition* is made upon a slate with a piece of white chalk. "*Qu'est-ce que monsieur a mange?*" Sometimes it is very difficult to remember, but it is necessary. Such honesty compels an exertion. It is all added up and for the two of us on this evening, or any other evening, it may come to nine *francs*, which is not much to pay for a good dinner.

Then, on this evening, and every other evening, we went on, back as we had come, round past the other side of Sacre-Coeur, past the statue of the Chevalier who was martyred for refusing to salute a procession (why he refused I have never found out, although I have asked everybody who has ever dined with me at the Cou-Cou) to the Cafe Savoyarde, the broad windows of which look out over pretty much all the Northeast of Paris, over a glittering labyrinth of lights set in an obscure sea of darkness. It was not far from here that Louise and Julien kept house when they were interrupted by Louise's mother, and it was looking down over these lights that they swore those eternal vows, ending with Louise's "*C'est une Feerie!*" and Julien's "Non, c'est la vie!" One always remembers these things and feels them at the Savoyarde as keenly as one did sometime in the remote past watching Mary Garden and Leon Beyle from the topmost gallery of the Opera-Comique after an hour and a half wait in the *queue* for one *franc* tickets (there were always people turned away from performances of *Louise* and so it was necessary to be there early; some other operas did not demand such punctuality). There is a terrace outside the Savoyarde, a tiny terrace, with just room for one man, who griddles *gaufrettes*, and three or four tiny tables with chairs. At one of these we sat that night (just as I had sat so many times before) and sipped our cognac.

It is difficult in an adventure to remember just when the departure comes, when one leaves the past and strides into the future, but I think that moment befell me in this cafe ... for it was the first time I had ever seen a cat there. He was a lazy, splendid animal. In New York he would have been an oddity, but in Paris there are many such beasts. Tawny he was and soft to the touch and of a hugeness. He was lying on the bar and as I stroked his coat he purred melifluously.... I stroked his warm fur and thought how I belonged to the mystic band (Gautier, Baudelaire, Merimee, all knew the secrets) of those who are acquainted with cats; it is a feeling of pride we have that differentiates us from the dog lovers, the pride of the appreciation of indifference or of conscious preference. And it was, I think, as I was stroking the cat that my past was smote away from me and I was projected into the adventure for, as I lifted the animal into my arms, the better to feel its warmth and softness, it sprang with strength and unsheathed claws out of my embrace, and soon was back on the bar again, "just as if nothing had happened." There was blood on my face. Madame, behind the bar, was apologetic but not chastening. "Il avait peur, *" she said. "*Il n'est pas mechant." The wound was not deep, and as I bent to pet the cat again he again purred. I had interfered with his habits and, as I discovered later, he had interfered with mine.

We decided to walk down the hill instead of riding down in the *finiculaire*, down the stairs which form another of the pictures in *Louise*, with the abutting houses, into the rooms of which one looks, conscious of prying. And you see the old in these interiors, making shoes, or preparing dinner, or the middle-aged going to bed, but the young one never sees in the houses in the summer.... It was early and we decided to dance; I thought of the Moulin de la Galette, which I had visited twice before. The Moulin de la Galette waves its gaunt arms in the air half way up the *butte* of Montmartre; it serves its purpose as a dance hall of the quarter. One meets the pretty little *Montmartroises* there and the young artists; the entrance fee is not exorbitant and one may drink a bock. And when I have been there, sitting at a small table facing the somewhat vivid mural decoration which runs the length of one wall, drinking my brown *bock*, I have remembered the story which Mary Garden once told me, how Albert Carre to celebrate the hundredth--or was it the twenty-fifth?--performance of *Louise*, gave a dinner there--so near to the scenes he had conceived--to Charpentier and how, surrounded by some of the most notable musicians and poets of France, the composer had suddenly fallen from the table, face downwards; he had starved himself so long to complete his masterpiece that food did not seem to nourish him. It was the end of a brilliant dinner. He was carried away ... to the Riviera; some said that he had lost his mind; some said that he was dying. Mary Garden herself did not know, at the time she first sang *Louise* in America, what had happened to him. But a little later the rumour that he was writing a trilogy was spread about and soon it was a known fact that at least one other part of the trilogy had been written, *Julien*; that lyric drama was produced and everybody knows the story of its failure. Charpentier, the natural philosopher and the poet of Montmartre, had said everything he had to say in *Louise*. As for the third play, one has heard nothing about that yet.

But on this evening the Moulin de la Galette was closed and then I remembered that it was open on Thursday and this was Wednesday. Is it Thursday, Saturday, and Sunday that the Moulin de la Galette is open? I think so. By this time we were determined to dance; but where? We had no desire to go to some stupid place, common to tourists, no such place as the Bal Tabarin lured us; nor did the Grelot in the Place Blanche, for we had been there a night or two before. The Elysee Montmartre (celebrated by George Moore) would be closed. Its *patron* followed the schedule of days adopted for the Galette.... To chance I turn in such dilemmas.... I consulted a small boy, who, with his companion, had been good enough to guide us through many winding streets to the Moulin. Certainly he knew of a *bal*. Would *monsieur* care to visit a *bal musette*? His companion was horrified. I caught the phrase "*mal frequente*." Our curiosity was aroused and we gave the signal to advance.

There were two grounds for my personal curiosity beyond the more obvious ones. I seemed to remember to have read somewhere that the ladies of the court of Louis XIV played the *musette*, which is French for bag-pipe. It was the fashionable instrument of an epoch and the *musettes* played by the *grandes dames* were elaborately decorated. The word in time slunk into the dictionaries of musical terms as descriptive of a drone bass. Many of Gluck's ballet airs bear the title, *Musette*. Perhaps the bass was even performed on a bag-pipe.... "*Mal frequente*" in Parisian *argot* has a variety of significations; in this particular instance it suggested *apaches* to me. A *bal*, for instance, attended by *cocottes*, *mannequins*, or *modeles*, could not be described as *mal frequente* unless one were speaking to a boarding school miss, for all the public *bals* in Paris are so attended. No, the words spoken to me, in this connection, could only mean *apaches*. The confusion of epochs began to invite my interest and I wondered, in my mind's eye, how a Louis XIV *apache* would dress, how he would be represented at a costume ball, and a picture of a ragged silk-betrousered person, flaunting a plaid-bellied instrument came to mind. An imagination often leads one violently astray.

The two urchins were marching us through street after street, one of them whistling that pleasing tune, Le lendemain elle etait souriante. Dark passage ways intervened between us and our destination: we threaded them. The cobble stones of the underfoot were not easy to walk on for my companion, shod in high-heels from the Place Vendome.... The urchins amused each other and us by capers on the way. They could have made our speed walking on their hands, and they accomplished at least a third of the journey this way. Of course, I deluged them with large round five and ten *centimes* pieces.

We arrived at last before a door in a short street near the Gare du Nord. Was it the Rue Jessaint? I do not know, for when, a year later, I attempted to re-find this *bal* it had disappeared.... We could hear the hum of the pipes for some paces before we turned the corner into the street, and never have pipes sounded in my ears with such a shrill significance of being somewhere they ought not to be, never but once, and that was when I had heard the piper who accompanies the dinner of the Governor of the Bahamas in Nassau. Marching round the porch of the Governor's Villa he played *The Blue Bells of Scotland* and God Save the King, but, hearing the sound from a distance through the interstices of the cocoa-palm fronds in the hot tropical night, I could only think of a Hindoo blowing the pipes in India, the charming of snakes.... So, as we turned the corner into the Rue Jessaint, I seemed to catch a faint glimpse of a scene on the lawn at Versailles.... Louis XIV--it was the epoch of Cinderella!

But it wasn't a bag-pipe at all. That we discovered when we entered the room, after passing through the bar in the front. The *bal* was conducted in a large hall at the back of the *maison*. In the doorway lounged an *agent de service*, always a guest at one of these functions, I found out later. There were rows of tables, long tables, with long wooden benches placed between them. One corner of the floor was cleared--not so large a corner either--for dancing, and on a small platform sat the strangest looking youth, like Peter Pan never to grow old, like the *Monna Lisa* a boy of a thousand years, without emotion or expression of any sort. He was playing an accordion; the bag-pipe, symbol of the *bal*, hung disused on the wall over his head. His accordion, manipulated with great skill, was augmented by sleigh-bells attached to his ankles in such a manner that a minimum of movement produced a maximum of effect; he further added to the complexity of sound and rhythm by striking a cymbal occasionally with one of his feet. The music was both rhythmic and ordered, now a waltz, now a tune in two-four time, but never faster or slower, and never ending ... except in the middle of each dance, for a brief few seconds, while the *patronne* collected a *sou* from each dancer, after which the dance proceeded. All the time we remained never did the musician smile, except twice, once briefly when I sent word to him by the waiter to order a *consommation* and once, at some length, when we departed. On these occasions the effect was almost emotionally illuminating, so inexpressive was the ordinary cast of his features. A strange lad; I like to think of him always sitting there, passively, playing the accordion and shaking his sleigh-bells. He suggested a static picture, a thing of always, but I know it is not so, for even the next summer he had disappeared along with the *bal* and now he may have been shot in the Battle of the Marne or he may have murdered his *gigolette* and been transported to one of the French penal colonies.... An apache, en musicien! ... black cloth around his throat, hair parted in the middle, *velours* trousers; a *vrai apache* I tell you, a cool, cunning creature, shredded with cocaine and absinthe, monotonous in his virtuosity, playing the accordion. He had begun before we arrived and he continued after we left. I like to think of him as always playing, but it is not so....

As for the dancers, they were of various kinds and sorts. The women had that air which gave them the stamp of a quarter; they wore loose *blouses*, tucked in plaid skirts, or dark blue skirts, or multi-coloured calico skirts (if you have seen the lithographs of Steinlen you may reconstruct the picture with no difficulty) and they danced in that peculiar fashion so much in vogue in the Northern

outskirts of Paris. The men seized them tightly and they whirled to
the inexorable music when it was a waltz, whirled and whirled, until
one thought of the Viennese and how they become as dervishes and
Japanese mice when one plays Johann Strauss. But in the dances in
two-four time their way was more our way, something between a
one-step, a mattchiche, and a tango, with strange fascinating steps of
their own devising, a folk-dance manner.... Yes, under their feet, the
dance became a real dance of the people and, when we entered into it,
our feet seemed heavy and our steps conventional, although we tried
to do what they did. (How they did laugh at us!) And the strange
youth emphasized the effect of folk-dancing by playing old chansons
de France *which he mingled with his repertory of* cafe-concert airs.
And there was achieved that wonderful thing (to an artist) a mixture
of *genres*--intriguing one's curiosity, awakening the most dormant
interest, and inspiring the dullest imagination.

This was my first night at a *bal musette* and my last in that year,
for shortly afterwards I left for Italy and in Italy one does not
dance. But the next season found me anxious to renew the adventure, to
again enjoy the pleasures of the *bal musette*. I have said I was
perhaps wrong in recalling the street as the Rue Jessaint, or perhaps
the old *maison* had disappeared. At any rate, when I searched I could
not find the *bal*, not even the bar. So again I appealed for help,
this time to a chauffeur, who drove me to the opposite side of the
city, to the *quartier* of the *Halles*.... And I was beginning to
think that the man had misunderstood me, or was stupid. "He will take
me to a cabaret, l'Ange Gabriel or"--and I rapidly revolved in my mind
the possibilities of this quarter where the *apaches* come to the
surface to feel the purse of the tourist, who buys drinks as he
listens to stories of murders, some of which have been committed, for
it is true that some of the real *apaches* go there (I know because my
friend Fernand did and it was in l'Ange Gabriel that he knocked all

the teeth down the throat of Angelique, *sa gigolette*. You may find the life of these creatures vividly and amusingly described in that amazing book of Charles-Henry Hirsch, "Le Tigre et Coquelicot" It is the only book I have read about the *apaches* of modern Paris that is worth its pages). But the idea of l'Ange Gabriel was not amusing to me this evening and I leaned forward to ask my chauffeur if he had it in mind to substitute another attraction for my desired *bal musette*. His reply was reassuring; it took the form of a gesture, the waving of a hand towards a small lighted globe depending over the door of a little *marchand de vin*. On this globe was painted in black letters the single word, *bal*. We were in the narrow Rue des Gravilliers--I was there for the first time--and the *bal* was the Bal des Gravilliers.

The bar is so small, when one enters, that there is no intimation of the really splendid aspect of the dancing room. For here there are two rooms separated by the dancing floor, two halls filled with tables, with long wooden benches between them. Benches also line the walls, which are white with a grey-blue frieze; the lighting is brilliant. The musicians play in a little balcony, and here there are two of them, an accordionist and a guitarist. The performer on the accordion is a *virtuoso*; he takes delight in winding florid ornament, after the manner of some brilliant singer impersonating Rosina in Il Barbiere, around the melodies he performs. As in the Rue Jessaint a *sou* is demanded in the middle of each dance. But there comparison must cease, for the life here is gayer, more of a character. The types are of the *Halles*.... There are strange exits....

A short woman enters; "elle s'avance en se balancant sur ses hanches comme une pouliche du haras de Cordoue"; she suggests an operatic Carmen in her swagger. She is slender, with short, dark hair, cropped *a la* Boutet de Monvel, and she flourishes a cigarette, the smoke

from which wreathes upward and obscures--nay makes more subtle--the
strange poignancy of her deep blue eyes. Her nose is of a snubness. It
is the *mome* Estelle, and as she passes down the narrow aisle,
between the tables, there is a stir of excitement.... The men raise
their eyes.... Edouard, *le petit*, flicks a *louis* carelessly
between his thumb and fore-finger, with the long dirty nails, and
then passes it back into his pocket. Do not mistake the gesture; it
is not made to entice the *mome*, nor is it a sign of affluence; it is
Edouard's means of demanding another *louis* before the night is up,
if it be only a "*louis de dix francs*." Estelle looks at him boldly;
there is no fear in her eyes; you can see that she would face death
with Carmen's calm if the Fates cut the thread to that effect.... The
music begins and Estelle dances with Carmella, *l'Arabe*. Edouard
glowers and pulls his little grey cap down tower.... It is a waltz....
Suddenly he is on the floor and Estelle is pressed close to his
body.... Carmella sits down. She smiles, and presently she is dancing
with Jean-Baptiste.... Estelle and Edouard are now whirling, whirling,
and all the while his dark eyes look down piercingly into her blue
eyes. The music stops. Estelle fumbles in her stocking for two *sous*.
Edouard lights a *Maryland*.

There is a newcomer tonight. (I am talking to the *agent de service*.)
She is of a youth and she is certainly from Brittany. I see her
sitting in a corner, waiting for something, trying to know. "She will
learn," says my friend, "She will learn to pay like the others." That
is the *gros* Pierre who regards her. He twirls his moustache and
considers, and in the end he lumbers to her and asks her to dance.
She is willing to do so, but the intensity of Pierre frightens her,
frightens and intrigues.... There is a sign on the wall that one must
not stamp one's feet, but no other prohibition.... He twists her
finger purposely as they whirl ... and whirl. She cowers. *Gros*
Pierre is very big and strong. "*T'es bath, mome*," I hear him say, as

they pass me by.... The dance over, he towers above her for a brief second before he swaggers out.... Estelle smiles. Her lips move and she speaks quickly to Edouard, *le petit*.... He does not listen. Why should he listen to his **gigolette**? She is wasting her time here anyway. He becomes impatient.... Carmella smiles across the room in a brief second of chance and Estelle answers the smile. Carmella holds up three fingers (it is now 1.30). Estelle nods her head quickly. The musicians are always playing, except in the middle of the dance when **madame, la patronne**, gathers in the **sous**.... Only from one she takes nothing.... He is twenty and very blonde and he is dancing with **Madame**.... Between dances she pays his **consommations**.... Estelle rises slowly and walks out while Carmella, *l'Arabe*, follows her with his eyes. Edouard, *le petit*, lights a **Maryland** and poises a **louis** between his thumb and fore-finger, the nails of which are long and dirty.... The music is always playing.... The little girl from Brittany is again alone in the corner. There is fear in her face. She is beginning to know. She summons her courage and walks to the door, on through.... The **agent de service** twirls his moustache and points after her. "She soon will know." I follow. She hesitates for a second at the street door and then starts towards the corner.... She reaches the corner and passes around it.... I hear a scream ... the sound of running footsteps ... the beat of a horse's hoofs ... the rolling of wheels on the cobble stones....

November 11, 1915.

Music and Cooking

"Give me some music,--music, moody food
Of us that trade in love."

Shakespeare's **Cleopatra**.

Music and Cooking

It is my firm belief that there is an intimate relationship between
the stomach and the ear, the saucepan and the crotchet, the mysteries
of Mrs. Rorer and the mysteries of Mme. Marchesi. It has even occurred
to me that one of the reasons our American composers are so barren in
ideas is because as a race we are not interested in cooking and
eating. Those countries in which music plays the greater part in the
national life are precisely those which are the most interested in the
culinary art. The food of Italy, the cooking, is celebrated; every
peasant in that sunny land sings, and the voices of some Italians have
reverberated around the world. The very melodies of Verdi and Rossini
are inextricably twined in our minds around memories of *ravioli* and
zabaglione. **Vesti la Giubba** is **spaghetti**. The composers of these
melodies and their interpreters alike cooked, ate, and drank with joy,
and so they composed and sang with joy too. Men with indigestion may
be able to write novels, but they cannot compose great music.... The
Germans spend more time eating than the people of any other country
(at least they did once). It is small occasion for wonder, therefore,
that they produce so many musicians. They are always eating, mammoth

plates heaped high with Bavarian cabbage, ***Koenigsberger Klopps***, ***Hasenpfeffer***, noodles, sauerkraut, ***Wiener Schnitzel*** ... drinking seidels of beer. They escort sausages with them to the opera. All the women have their skirts honeycombed with capacious pockets, in which they carry substantial lunches to eat while Isolde is deceiving King Mark. Why, the very principle of German music is based on a theory of well-fed auditors. The voluptuous scores of Richard Wagner, Richard Strauss, Max Schillings and Co. were not written for skinny, ill-nourished wights. Even Beethoven demands flesh and bone of his hearers. The music of Bach is directly aimed against the doctrine of asceticism. "The German capacity for feeling emotion in music has developed to the same extent as the capacity of the German stomach for containing food," writes Ernest Newman, "but in neither the one case nor the other has there been a corresponding development in refinement of perceptions. German sentimental music is not quite as gross as German food and German feeding, but it comes very near to it sometimes.... 'The Germans do not taste,' said Montaigne, 'they gulp.' As with their food, so with the emotions of their music. So long as they get them in sufficient mass, of the traditional quality, and with the traditional pungent seasoning, they are content to leave piquancy and variety of effect to others."... Once in Munich in a second storey window of the Bayerischebank I saw a small boy, about ten years old, sitting outside on the sill, washing the panes of glass. Opposite him on the same sill a dachshund reposed on her paws, regarding her master affectionately. Between the two stood a half-filled toby of foaming Lowenbrau, which, from time to time, the lad raised to his lips, quaffing deep draughts. And when he set the pot down he whistled the first subject of Beethoven's ***Fifth Symphony***. On Sunday afternoons, in the gardens which invariably surround the Munich breweries, the happy mothers, who gather to listen to the band play while they drink beer, frequently replenish the empty nursing bottles of their offspring at the taps from which flows the deep brown beverage.... The food of the French is highly artificial, delicately

prepared and served, and flavoured with infinite art: vol au vent a
la reine **and Massenet,** petits pois a l'etuvee **and Gounod,** oeuf
Ste. Clotilde and Cesar Franck, all strike the tongue and the ear
quite pleasantly. Des Esseintes and his liqueur symphony were the
inventions of a Frenchman.... Hungarian goulash and Hungarian
rhapsodies are certainly designed to be taken in conjunction....
Russian music tastes of **kascha** and **bortsch** and vodka. The happy,
hearty eaters of Russia, the drunken, sodden drinkers of Russia are
reflected in the scores of **Boris Godunow** and **Petrouchka**.... In
England we find that the great English meat pasties and puddings
appeared in the same century with the immortal Purcell.... But in
America we import our cooks ... and our music. As a race we do not
like to cook. We scarcely like to eat. We certainly do not enjoy
eating. We will never have a national music until we have national
dishes and national drinks and until we like good food. It is
significant that our national drinks at present are mixed drinks, the
ingredients of which are foreign. It is doubly significant that that
section of the country which produces chicken **a la Maryland**, corn
bread, beaten biscuit, mint juleps, and New Orleans fizzes has
furnished us with the best of such music as we can boast. Maine has
offered us no **Suwanee River**; we owe no **Swing Low, Sweet Chariot** to
Nebraska. The best of our ragtime composers are Jews, a race which
regards eating and cooking of sufficient importance to include rules
for the preparation and disposition of food in its religious tenets.

Most musicians and those who enjoy listening to music, like to eat
(this does not mean that people who like to eat always desire to
listen to music at the same time, but nowadays one has little choice
in the matter); what is more pregnant, most of them like to cook. We
may include even the music critics, one of whom (Henry T. Finck) has
written a book about such matters. The others eat ... and expand.
James Huneker devotes sixteen pages of "The New Cosmopolis" to the
"maw of the monster." And as H. L. Mencken has pointed out, "The

Pilsner motive runs through the book from cover to cover." Dinners are
constantly being given for the musicians and critics to meet and talk
over thirteen courses with wine. You may read Mr. Krehbiel's glowing
accounts of the dinner given to Adelina Patti (a dinner referred to in
Joseph Hergesheimer's lyric novel, "The Three Black Pennys") on the
occasion of her twenty-fifth anniversary as a singer, of the dinner to
Marcella Sembrich to mark her retirement from the opera stage, and of
a dinner to Teresa Carreno when she proposed a toast to her three
husbands.... Go to the opera house and observe the lady singers, with
their ample bosoms and their broad hips, the men with their expansive
paunches ... and use your imagination. Why is it, when a singer is
interviewed for a newspaper, that she invariably finds herself tired
of hotel food and wants an apartment of her own, where she can cook to
her stomach's content? Why are the musical journals and the Sunday
supplements of the newspapers always publishing pictures of contralti
with their sleeves rolled back to the elbows, their Poiret gowns
(cunningly and carefully exhibited nevertheless) covered with aprons,
baking bread, turning omelettes, or preparing clam broth Uncle Sam?
You, my reader, have surely seen these pictures, but it has perhaps
not occurred to you to conjure up a reason for them.

Edgar Saltus says: "A perfect dinner should resemble a concert. As the
morceaux succeed each other, so, too, should the names of the
composers." Few dinners in New York may be regarded as concerts and
still fewer restaurants may be looked upon as concert halls, except,
unfortunately, in the literal sense. However, if you can find a
restaurant where opera singers and conductors eat you may be sure it
is a good one. Huneker describes the old Lienau's, where William
Steinway, Anton Seidl, Theodore Thomas, Scharwenka, Joseffy, Lilli
Lehmann, Max Heinrich, and Victor Herbert used to gather. Follow
Alfred Hertz and you will be in excellent company in a double sense.
Then watch him consume a plateful of Viennese pastry. If you have ever
seen Emmy Destinn or Feodor Chaliapine eat you will feel that justice

has been done to a meal. I once sat with the Russian bass for twelve hours, all of which time he was eating or drinking. He began with six plates of steaming onion soup (cooked with cheese and toast). The old New Year's eve festivities at the Gadski-Tauschers' resembled the storied banquets of the middle ages.... Boars' heads, meat pies, **salade macedoine**, **coeur de palmier**, **hollandaise** were washed down with magnums and quarts of Irroy brut, 1900, Pol Roger, Chambertin, graceful Bohemian crystal goblets of Liebfraumilch and Johannisberger Schloss-Auslese. Mary Garden once sent a jewelled gift to the **chef** at the Ritz-Carlton in return for a superb fish sauce which he had contrived for her. H. E. Krehbiel says that Brignoli "probably ate as no tenor ever ate before or since--ravenously as a Prussian dragoon after a fast." **Peche Melba** has become a stable article on many menus in many cities in many lands. Agnes G. Murphy, in her biography of Mme. Melba, says that one day the singer, Joachim, and a party of friends stopped at a peasant's cottage near Bergamo, where they were regaled with such delicious macaroni that Melba persuaded her friends to return another day and wait while the peasant taught her the exact method of preparing the dish. In at least one New York restaurant **oeuf Toscanini** is to be found on the bill. I have heard Olive Fremstad complain of the cooking in this hotel in Paris, or that hotel in New York, or the other hotel in Munich, and when she found herself in an apartment of her own she immediately set about to cook a few special dishes for herself.

Two musicians I know not only keep restaurants in New York, but actually prepare the dinners themselves. One of them is at the same time a singer in the Metropolitan Opera Company. Have you seen Bernard Begue standing before his cook stove preparing food for his patrons? His huge form, clad in white, viewed through the open doorway connecting the dining room with the kitchen, almost conceals the great stove, but occasionally you can catch sight of the pots and pans, the **casseroles** of **pot-au-feu**, the roasting chicken, the filets of sole, all the ingredients of a dinner, ***cuisine bourgeoise*** ... and after dining, you can hear Begue sing the Uncle-priest in Madama Butterfly at the Opera House.

Or have you seen Giacomo (and have not Meyerbeer and Puccini been bearers of this name?) Pogliani turning from the ***spaghetti*** theme chromatically to that of the ***risotto***, the most succulent and appetizing ***risotto*** to be tasted this side of Bonvecchiati's in Venice ... or the ***polenta*** with ***funghi***.... But, best of all, the roasts, and were it not that the Prince Troubetskoy is a vegetarian you would fancy that he came to Pogliani's for these viands. And it must not be forgotten that this supreme cook is--or was--a bassoon player of the first rank, that he is a graduate of the Milan Conservatory. The bassoon is a difficult instrument. It is sometimes called the "comedian of the orchestra," but there are few who can play it at all, still fewer who can play it well. Bassoonists are highly paid and they are in demand. Walter Damrosch used to say that when he was engaging a bassoon player he would ask him to play a passage from the bassoon part in ***Scheherazade***. If he could play that, he could play anything else written for his instrument. Pogliani gave up the bassoon for the fork, spoon, and saucepan. Like Prospero he buried his magic wand and in Viafora's cartoon the instrument lies idle in the cobwebs.

Charles Santley's "Reminiscences" and "Student and Singer" are full of references to food: "ox-hearts, stuffed with onions," "a joint of meat, well cooked, with a bright brown crust which prevented the juices escaping," "a splendid shoulder of mutton, a picture to behold, and a ***peas pudding***," and "whaffles" are a few of the dishes referred to with enthusiasm. In America a newspaper gravely informed its readers that "Santley says squash pie is the best thing to sing on he knows!" Santley was a true pantophagist, but he was worsted in his first encounter with the American oyster: "I had often heard of the celebrated American oyster, which half a dozen people had tried to swallow without success, and was anxious to learn if the story were founded on fact. Cummings conducted me to a cellar in Broadway, where, upon his order, a waiter produced two plates, on which were half a dozen objects, about the size and shape of the sole of an ordinary lady's shoe, on each of which lay what appeared to me to be a very bilious tongue, accompanied by smaller plates containing shredded white cabbage raw. I did not admire the look of the repast, but I never discard food on account of looks. I took up an oyster and tried to get it into my mouth, but it was of no use; I tried to ram it in with the butt-end of the fork, but all to no purpose, and I had to drop it, and, to the great indignation of the waiter, paid and left the oysters for him to dispose of as he might like best. I presume those oysters are eaten, but I cannot imagine by whom; I have rarely seen a mouth capable of the necessary expansion. I soon found out that there were plenty of delicious oysters in the States within the compass of ordinary jaws."

J. H. Mapleson says in his "Memoirs" that at the Opera at Lodi, where he made his debut as a tenor, refreshments of all kinds were served to the audience between the acts and every box was furnished with a little kitchen for cooking macaroni and baking or frying pastry. The wine of the country was drunk freely, not out of glasses, but "in classical fashion--from bowls." Mapleson also tells us that Del Puente was a "very tolerable cook." On one trying occasion he prepared macaroni for his impressario. Michael Kelly declares that the sight of Signor St. Giorgio entering a fruit shop to eat peaches, nectarines, and a pineapple, was really what stimulated him to study for a career on the stage. "While my mouth watered, I asked myself why, if I assiduously studied music, I should not be able to earn money enough to lounge about in fruit-shops, and eat peaches and pineapples as well as Signor St. Giorgio...."

Lillian Russell is a good cook. I can recommend her recipe for the preparation of mushrooms: "Put a lump of butter in a chafing dish (or a saucepan) and a slice of Spanish onion and the mushrooms minus the stems; let them simmer until they are all deliciously tender and the juice has run from them--about twenty minutes should be enough--then add a cupful of cream and let this boil. As a last touch squeeze in the juice of a lemon." When Luisa Tetrazzini was going mad with a flute in our vicinity she varied the monotony of her life by sending pages of her favourite recipes to the Sunday yellow press. Unfortunately, I neglected to make a collection of this series. A passion for cooking caused the death of Naldi, a buffo singer of the early Nineteenth Century. Michael Kelly tells the story: "His ill stars took him to Paris, where, one day, just before dinner, at his friend Garcia's house, in the year 1821, he was showing the method of cooking by steam, with a portable apparatus for that purpose; unfortunately, in consequence of some derangement of the machinery, an explosion took place, by which he was instantaneously killed." Almost everybody knows some story or other about a *virtuoso*, trapped into dining and asked to perform after dinner by his host. Kelly relates one of the first: "Fischer, the great oboe player, whose minuet was then all the rage ... being very much pressed by a nobleman to sup with him after the opera, declined the invitation, saying that he was usually much fatigued, and made it a rule never to go out after the evening's performance. The noble lord would, however, take no denial, and assured Fischer that he did not ask him professionally, but merely for the gratification of his society and conversation. Thus urged and encouraged, he went; he had not, however, been many minutes in the house of the consistent nobleman, before his lordship approached him, and said, 'I hope, Mr. Fischer, you have brought your oboe in your pocket.'--'No, my Lord,' said Fischer, 'my oboe never sups.' He turned on his heel, and instantly left the house, and no persuasion could ever induce him to return to it." You perhaps have heard rumours that Giuseppe Campanari prefers *spaghetti* to Mozart, especially when he cooks it himself. When this baritone was a member of the Metropolitan Opera Company his paraphernalia for preparing his favourite food went everywhere with him on tour. Heinrich Conried (or was it Maurice Grau?) once tried to take advantage of this weakness, according to a story often related by the late Algernon St. John Brenon. Campanari was to appear as Kothner in **Die Meistersinger**, a character with no singing to do after the first act, although he appears in the procession in the third act. The singer told his impressario that he saw no reason why he should remain to the end and explained that he would leave his costume for a chorus man to don to represent him in the final episode. "What would the Master say?" demanded Conried, wringing his hands. "Would he approve of such a proceeding? No. That would not be truth! That would not be art!" Campanari was obdurate. The Herr Direktor became reflective. He was silent for a moment and then he continued: "If you will stay for the last act you will find in your room a little supper, a bottle of wine, and a box of cigars, which you may consume while you are waiting." In sooth when Campanari entered his dressing room after the first act of Wagner's comic opera he found that his director had kept his word.... The baritone ate the supper, drank the wine, put the cigars in his pocket ... and went home!

If some singers are good cooks it does not follow that all good cooks are singers. Benjamin Lumley, in his "Reminiscences of the Opera," tells the sad story of the Countess of Cannazaro's cook, which should serve as a lesson to housemaids who are desirous of becoming moving picture stars. "This worthy man, excellent no doubt as a **chef**, took it into his head that he was a vocalist of the highest order, and that he only wanted opportunity to earn musical distinction. His strange fancy came to the knowledge of Rubini, and it was arranged that a performance should take place in the morning, in which the cook's talent should be fairly tested. Certainly every chance was afforded him. Not only was he encouraged by Rubini and Lablache (whose gravity on the occasion was wonderful), but by a few others, Costa included, as instrumentalists. The failure was miserable, ridiculous, as everybody expected." Frederick Crowest describes a certain Count Castel de Maria who had a spit that played tunes, "and so regulated and indicated the condition of whatever was hung upon it to roast. By a singular mechanical contrivance this wonderful spit would strike up an appropriate tune whenever a joint had hung sufficiently long on its particular roast. Thus, *Oh! the roast beef of Old England*, when a sirloin had turned and hung its appointed time. At another air, a leg of mutton, *a l'Anglaise* would be found excellent; while some other tune would indicate that a fowl *a la Flamande* was cooked to a nicety and needed removal from the fowl roast."

To Crowest, too, I am indebted for a list of beverages and eatables which certain singers held in superstitious awe as capable of refreshing their voices. Formes swore by a pot of good porter and Wachtel is said to have trusted to the yolk of an egg beaten up with sugar to make sure of his high Cs. The Swedish tenor, Labatt, declared that two salted cucumbers gave the voice the true metallic ring. Walter drank cold black coffee during a performance; Southeim took snuff and cold lemonade; Steger, beer; Niemann, champagne, slightly warmed, (Huneker once saw Niemann drinking cocktails from a beer glass; he sang Siegmund at the opera the next night); Tichatschek, mulled claret; Rubgam drank mead; Nachbaur ate bonbons; Arabanek believed in Gampoldskirchner wine. Mlle. Brann-Brini took beer and *cafe au lait*, but she also firmly believed in champagne and would never dare venture the great duet in the fourth act of *Les Huguenots* without a bottle of Moet Cremant Rose. Giardini being asked his opinion of Banti, previous to her arrival in England, said: "She is the first singer in Italy and drinks a bottle of wine every day." Malibran believed in the efficacy of porter. She made her last appearances in opera in Balfe's *Maid of Artois* during the fall of 1836 in London. On the first night she was in anything but good physical condition and the author of "Musical Recollections of the Last Half-Century" tells how she pulled herself through: "She remembered that an immense trial awaited her in the finale of the third act; and finding her strength giving way, she sent for Mr. Balfe and Mr. Bunn, and told them that unless they did as they were bid, after all the previous success, the end might result in failure; but she said, 'Manage to let me have a pot of porter somehow or other before I have to sing, and I will get you an encore which will bring down the house.' How to manage this was difficult; for the scene was so set that it seemed scarcely possible to hand her up 'the pewter' without its being witnessed by the audience. After much consultation, Malibran having been assured that her wish should be fulfilled, it was arranged that the pot of porter should be handed up to her through a trap in the stage at the moment when Jules had thrown himself on her body, supposing that life had fled; and Mr. Templeton was drilled into the manner in which he should so manage to conceal the necessary arrangement, that the audience would never suspect what was going on. At the right moment a friendly hand put the foaming pewter through the stage, to be swallowed at a draught, and success was won!... Malibran, however, had not overestimated her own strength. She knew that it wanted but this fillip to carry her through. She had resolved to have an encore, and she had it, in such a fashion as made the roof of 'Old Drury' ring as it had never rung before. On the repetition of the opera and afterwards, a different arrangement of the stage was made, and a property calabash containing a pot of porter was used; but although the same result was constantly won, Malibran always said it was not half so 'nice,' nor did her anything like the good it would have done if she could only have had it out of the pewter." Clara Louise Kellogg in her very lively "Memoirs" publishes a similar tale of another singer: "It was told of Grisi that when she was growing old and severe exertion told on her she always, after her fall as Lucrezia Borgia, drank a glass of beer sent up to her through the floor, lying with her back half turned to the audience." Miss Kellogg complains of the breaths of the tenors she sang with: "Stigelli usually exhaled an aroma of lager beer; while the good Mazzoleni invariably ate from one to two pounds of cheese the day he was to sing. He said it strengthened his voice. Many of them affected garlic." It is necessary, of course, that a singer should know what foods agree with him. He must keep himself in excellent physical condition: small wonder that many artists are superstitious in this regard.

Charles Santley, who was so fond of eating and drinking himself, offers some excellent advice on the subject in "Student and Singer": "How the voice is produced or where, except that it is through the passage of the throat, is unimportant; it is reasonable to say that the passage must be kept clear, otherwise the sound proceeding from it will not be clear. I have known many instances of singers undergoing very disagreeable operations on their throats for chronic diseases of various descriptions; now, my observation and experience assure me that, in ninety-nine cases out of a hundred, the root of the evil is chronic inattention to food and raiment. It is a common thing to hear a singer say, 'I never touch such-and-such food on the days I sing.' My dear young friend, unless you are an absolute idiot, you would not partake of anything on the days you sing which might disagree with you, or over-tax your digestive powers; it is on the days you do not sing you ought more particularly to exercise your judgment and self-denial. I do not offer the pinched-up pilgarlic who dines off a wizened apple and a crust of bread as a model for imitation; at the same time, I warn you seriously against following the example of the gobbling glutton who swallows every dish that tempts his palate."

Rossini, after he had composed *Guillaume Tell*, retired. He was thirty-seven, a man in perfect health, and he lived thirty-nine years longer, to the age of seventy-six, yet he never wrote another opera, hardly indeed did he dip his pen in ink at all. These facts have seriously disconcerted his biographers, who are at a loss to assign reasons for his actions. W. F. Apthorp gives us an ingenious explanation in "The Opera Past and Present." He says that after *Tell* Rossini's pride would not allow him to return to his earlier Italian manner, while the hard work needed to produce more *Tells* was more than his laziness could stomach.... Perhaps, but it must be remembered that Rossini did not retire to his library or his music room, but to his kitchen. The simple explanation is that he preferred cooking to composing, a fact easy to believe (I myself vastly prefer cooking to writing). He could cook *risotto* better than any one else he knew. He was dubbed a "hippopotamus in trousers," and for six years before he died he could not see his toes, he was so fat. Sir Arthur Sullivan relates an anecdote which shows that Rossini was conscious of his grossness. Once in Paris Sullivan introduced Chorley to Rossini, when the Italian said, "Je vois, avec plaisir, que monsieur n'a pas de ventre." Chorley indeed was noticeably slender. Rossini could write more easily, so his biographers tell us, when he was under the influence of champagne or some light wine. His provision merchant once begged him for an autographed portrait. The composer gave it to him with the inscription, "To my stomach's best friend." The tradesman used this souvenir as an advertisement and largely increased his business thereby, as such a testimonial from such an acknowledged epicure had a very definite value. J. B. Weckerlin asserts that when Rossini dined at the Rothschild's he first went to the kitchen to pay his respects to the *chef*, to look over the menu, and even to discuss the various dishes, after which he ascended to the drawing room to greet the family of the rich banker. Mme. Alboni told Weckerlin that Rossini had dedicated a piece of music to the Rothschild's *chef*.

Anfossi, we are informed, could compose only when he was surrounded by smoking fowls and Bologna sausages; their fumes seemed to inflame his imagination, to feed his muse; his brain was stimulated first through his nose and then through his stomach. When Gluck wrote music he betook himself to the open fields, accompanied by at least two bottles of champagne. Salieri told Michael Kelly that a comic opera of Gluck's being performed at the Elector Palatine's theatre, at Schwetzingen, his Electoral Highness was struck with the music, and inquired who had composed it; on being informed that he was an honest German who loved *old wine*, his Highness immediately ordered him a tun of Hock. Beethoven, on the contrary, seems to have fed on his thoughts occasionally, although there is evidence that he was not only a good eater but also a good cook (the mothers of both Beethoven and Schubert were cooks in domestic service). There is a story related of him that about the time he was composing the **Sixth Symphony** he walked into a Viennese restaurant and ordered dinner. While it was being prepared, he became involved in thought, and when the waiter returned to serve him, he said: "Thank you, I have dined!" laid the price of the dinner on the table, and took his departure. Gretry, too, lost his appetite when he was composing. There are numerous references to eating and drinking in Mendelssohn's letters. His particular preferences, according to Sir George Grove, were for rice milk and cherry pie. Dussek was a famous eater, and it is said that his ruling passion eventually killed him. His patron, the Prince of Benevento, paid the composer eight hundred napoleons a year, with a free table for three persons, at which, as a matter of fact, one person usually presided. A musical historian tells us that in the summer of 1797 he was dining with three friends at the Ship Tavern in Greenwich, when the waiter came and laid a cloth for one person at the next table, placing thereon a dish of boiled eels, one of fried flounders, a bowled fowl, a dish of veal cutlets, and a couple of tarts. Then Dussek entered and made away with the lot, leaving but the bones! In W. T. Parke's "Musical Memoirs" justice is done to the appetite of one C. F. Baumgarten, for many years leader of the band and composer at Covent Garden Theatre. Once at supper after the play he and a friend ate a full-grown hare between them. He would never condescend to drink out of anything but a quart pot. On one occasion, at the request of his friends, Baumgarten was weighed before and after dinner. There was eight pounds difference! William Shield, the composer who wrote many operas for Covent Garden Theatre, beginning aptly enough with one called *The Flitch of Bacon*, was something of an eater. Parke tells how at a dinner one evening there was a brace of partridges. The hostess handed Shield one of these to carve and absent-mindedly he set to and finished it, while the other guests were forced to make shift with the other partridge. Handel was a great eater. He was called the "Saxon Giant," as a tribute to his genius, but the phrase might have had a satirical reference to his enormous bulk. Intending to dine one day at a certain tavern, he ordered beforehand a dinner for three. At the hour appointed he sat down to the table and expressed astonishment that the dinner was not brought up. The waiter explained that he would begin serving when the company arrived. "Den pring up de tinner brestissimo," replied Handel, "I am de gombany." Lulli never forsook the *casserole*. Paganini was as good a cook as he was a violinist. Parke tells a story of Weichsell, not too celebrated a musician, but the father of Mrs. Billington and Charles Weichsell, the violinist: "He would occasionally supersede the labours of his cook, and pass a whole day in preparing his favourite dish, rump-steaks, for the stewing pan; and after the delicious viand had been placed on the dinner-table, together with early green peas of high price, if it happened that the sauce was not to his liking he has been known to throw rump-steaks, and green peas, and all, out of the window, whilst his wife and children thought themselves fortunate in not being thrown after them."

Is there a cooking theme in *Siegfried* to describe Mime's brewing? Lavignac and others, who have listed the *Ring motive*, have neglected to catalogue it, but it is mentioned by Old Fogy. Practically a whole act is taken up in *Louise* with the preparation for and consumption of a dinner. Scarpia eats in *Tosca* and the heroine kills him with a table knife. There is much talk of food in *Hansel und Gretel* and there is a supper in *The Merry Wives of Windsor*. There are drinking songs in **Don Giovanni**, **Lucrezia Borgia**, **Hamlet**, **La Traviata**, **Girofle-Girofla**.... The reference to whiskey and soda in Madama Butterfly is celebrated. J. E. Cox, the author of "Musical Recollections," describes Herr Pischek in the supper scene of Don Giovanni as "out-heroding Herod by swallowing glass after glass of champagne like a sot, and gnawing the drumstick of a fowl, which he held across his mouth with his fingers, just as any of his own middle-class countrymen may be seen any day of the week all the year round at the **mit-tag** or **abend-essen** feeding at one of their largely frequented **tables-d'hote**." Eating or drinking on the stage is always fraught with danger, as Charles Santley once discovered during Papageno's supper scene in **The Magic Flute**: "The supper which Tamino commands for the hungry Papageno consisted of pasteboard imitations of good things, but the cup contained real wine, a small draught of which I found refreshing on a hot night in July, amid the dust and heat of the stage. On the occasion in question I was putting the cup to lips, when I heard somebody call to me from the wings; I felt very angry at the interruption, and was just about to swallow the wine when I heard an anxious call not to drink. Suspecting something was wrong, I pretended to drink, and deposited the cup on the table. Immediately after the scene I made inquiries about the reason for the caution I received, and was informed that as each night the carpenters, who had no right to it, finished what remained of the wine before the property men, whose perquisite it was, could lay hold of the cup, the latter, to give their despoilers a lesson, had mingled castor-oil with my drink!"

A young husband of my acquaintance once bemoaned to me the fact that his wife seemed destined to become a great singer. "She is such a remarkable cook!" he explained to account for his despondency. I reassured him: "She will cook with renewed energy when she begins to sing **Sieglinde** and **Tosca**.... She will practise **Vissi d'Arte** over the gumbo soup and **Du herstes Wunder**! while the Frankfurters are sizzling. Her trills, her chromatic scales, and her ***messa di voce*** will come right in the kitchen; she will equalize her scale and learn to breathe correctly bending over the oven. It is even likely that she will improve her knowledge of ***portamento*** while she is washing dishes. When she can prepare a succulent roast suckling pig she will be able to sing ***Ocean, thou mighty monster***! and she will understand ***Abscheulicher*** when she understands the mysteries of old-fashioned strawberry shortcake. If you hear her shrieking ***Suicidio***! invoking Agamemnon, or appealing to the ***Casta Diva*** among the kettles and pots be not alarmed.... For the love you bear of good food, man, do not discourage your wife's ambition. The more she loves to sing, the better she will cook!"

July 17, 1917.

An Interrupted Conversation

"We can never depend upon any right adjustment of emotion to circumstance."

Max Beerbohm.

An Interrupted Conversation

Ordinarily one does not learn things about oneself from Edmund Gosse, but my discovery that I am a Pyrrhonist is due to that literary man. A Pyrrhonist, says Mr. Gosse, is "one who doubts whether it is worth while to struggle against the trend of things. The man who continues to cross the road leisurely, although the cyclists' bells are ringing, is a Pyrrhonist--and in a very special sense, for the ancient philosopher who gives his name to the class made himself conspicuous by refusing to get out of the way of careering chariots." Now the most unfamiliar friend I have ever walked with knows my extreme impassivity at the corners of streets, remembers the careless attitude with which I saunter from kerb to kerb, whether it be across the Grand Boulevard, Piccadilly, or Fifth Avenue. Only once has this nonchalant defiance of traffic caused me to come to even temporary grief; that was on the last night of the year 1913, when, in crossing Broadway, I became entangled, God knows how, in the wheels of a swiftly passing vehicle, and found myself, top hat and all, in the most ignominious position before I was well aware of what had really happened. Then a policeman stooped over me, book and pencil in hand, and another held the chauffeur of the victorious taxi-cab at bay some yards further up the street. But I was not hurt and I waved them all away with a magnanimous gesture.... It is owing to this habit of mine that I often make interesting *rencontres* in the middle of streets. It accounts, in fact, for my running, quite absent-mindedly, plump into Dickinson Sitgreaves, who is more American than his name sounds, one August day in Paris.

It was one of those charming days which make August perhaps the most delightful month to spend in Paris, although the facts are not known to tourists. Many a sly French pair, however, bored with Trouville, or the season at Aix, take advantage of the allurements of a Paris August to return surreptitiously to the boulevards. On this particular day almost all the seduction of an October day was in the air, a splendid dull warm-cool crispness, which filtered down through the faded chestnut leaves from the sunlight, and left pale splotches of purple

and orange on the **trottoirs** ... a really marvellous day, which I was
spending in that most excellent occupation in Paris of gazing into
shops and, passing cafes, staring into the faces of those who sat on
the **terrasses**.... But this is an occupation for one alone; so, when
I met Sitgreaves, we joined a **terrasse** ourselves. We were near the
Napolitain and there he and I sat down and began to talk as only we
two can talk together after long separation. He explained in the
beginning how I had interrupted him.... There was a **fille**, some
little Polish beauty who had captivated his senses a day or so before,
brought to him quite by accident in an hotel where the **patron**
furnished his clients with such pleasure as the town and his address
book afforded.... I knew the **patron** myself, a fluent, amusing sort
of person, who had been a **cuirassier** and who resembled Mayol ... a
cafe-concert proprietor of an hotel.... It was his boast that he had
never disappointed a client and it is certain that he would promise
anything. Some have said that his stock in trade was one pretty girl,
who assumed costumes, ages, hair, and accents, to please whatever
demand was made upon her, but this I do not believe. There must have
been at least two of them. The Grand Duchess Anastasia, it was
rumoured, had dined with Marcel at one time, in his little hotel, and
certainly one king had been seen to go there, and one member of the
English royal family, but Marcel remained simple and obliging.

"When will you look up the little **Polonaise**?" I asked, as we sipped
Amer Picon and stared with fresh interest at each new boot and ankle
that passed. Paris in August is like another place in May.

"Why don't you come along?" queried Sitgreaves in reply, "and we could
go at once.... Oh, I know that you are in no mood for pleasure. You
see the point is that I shall have to wait. Marcel will have to send
for the **fille**. It is a bore to wait in a room with red curtains and
a picture of **Amour et Psyche** on the walls.... What have you been

doing?" He paid the ***consommation*** and started to leave without
waiting for a reply, because he knew of my complaisance. I rose with
him and we walked down the boulevard.

"What is there to do in Paris in August but to enjoy oneself?" I
asked. "I have made friends with an ***apache*** and his ***gigolette***. We
eat bread and cheese and drink bad wine on the fortifications.... In
the afternoon I walk. Sometimes I go to the Luxembourg gardens to hear
the band bray sad music, or to watch the little boys play ***diavolo***,
or sail their tiny boats about the fountain pond; sometimes I walk
quite silently up the Avenue Gabriel, with its ***triste*** line of trees,
and dream that I am a Grand Duke; in the evening there are again the
terrasses of the cafes, dinner in Montmartre at the Clou, or the
Cou-Cou, a ***revue*** at La Cigale, but it is all governed, my day and my
night, by what happens and by whom I meet.... Have you seen Jacques
Blanche's portrait of Nijinsky?"

"I think it is Picasso that interests me now," Sitgreaves was saying.
"He puts wood and pieces of paper into his composition; architecture,
that's what it is.... I don't go to Blanche's any more. It's too
delightfully perfect, the atmosphere there.... The books are by all
the famous writers, and they are all dedicated to Blanche; the
pictures are all of the great men of today, and they are all painted
by Blanche; the music is played by the best musicians.... Do you know,
I think Blanche is the one man who has made a successful profession of
being an amateur--unless one excepts Robert de la Condamine.... You
can scarcely call a man who does so much a dilettante. Yes, I think he
is an amateur in the best sense."

"I met the Countess of Jena there the other day," I responded. "She
had scarcely left the room before three people volunteered, sans
rancune, to tell her story. She is a devout Catholic, and her husband
contrived in some way to substitute a spy for the priest in the

confessional. He acquired an infinite amount of information, but it didn't do him any good. She is so witty that every one invites her everywhere in spite of her reputation, and he is left to dine alone at the Meurice. Dull men simply are not tolerated in Paris.

"It was at Blanche's last year that I met George Moore," I continued. "You know I have just seen him in London. He is at work on The Apostle, making a novel of it, to be called 'The Brook Kerith.'... For a time he thought of finishing it up as a play because a novel meant a visit to Palestine and that was distasteful to him, but it finally became a novel. He went to Palestine and stayed six weeks, just long enough to find a monastery and to study the lay of the country. For he says, truly enough, that one cannot imagine landscapes; one does not know whether there is a high or low horizon. There may be a brook which all the characters must cross. It is necessary to see these things. Besides he had to find a monastery.... He told me of his thrill when he discovered an order of monks living on a narrow ledge of cliff, with 500 feet sheer rise and descent above and below it ... and when he had found this his work was done and he returned to England to write the book, a reaction, for he told me that he was getting tired of being personal in literature. The book will exhibit a conflict between two types: Christ, the disappointed mystic, and Paul; Christ, who sees that there is no good to be served in saving the world by his death, and Paul, full of hope, idealism, and illusions. It is the drama of the conflict between the nature which is affected by externals and that which is not, he told me."

"It's a subject for Anatole France," said Sitgreaves. "Moore, in my opinion, is not a novelist. His great achievements are his memoirs. I was interested in 'Evelyn Innes' and 'Esther Waters,' but something was lacking. There is nothing lacking in the three volumes of 'Hail and Farewell.' They grow in interest. Moore has found his ***metier***."

"But he insists," I explained, before the door of the little hotel, "that 'Hail and Farewell' is a novel. He is infuriated when some one suggests that it is a book after the manner of, say, 'The Reminiscences of Lady Randolph Churchill.'..."

We entered and walked up the little staircase.

"Do you mean that the incidents are untrue?"

We were at the door of the **concierge** and there stood Marcel, his apron spread neatly over his ample paunch. It was early in the afternoon and the room beyond him, sometimes filled with possibilities for customers, was empty.

"***Ah, monsieur est revenu!***" he exclaimed in his piping voice. "C'est pour la petite Polonaise sans doute que monsieur revient?"

"***Oui***," answered Sitgreaves, "***faut-il attendre longtemps?***"

"Mais non, monsieur, un petit moment. Elle habite en face. Je vais envoyer le garcon la chercher tout de suite. Et pour monsieur, votre ami?"

"***Je ne desire rien***," I replied.

Marcel bowed humbly.... "***Comme monsieur voudra.***" Then a doubt assailed him. "Peut-etre que la petite Polonaise vous suffira a tous les deux?"

"***Jamais de la vie!***" I shouted, "Flute, Mercure, allez! Je suis puceau!"

Marcel was equal to this. "***Et ta soeur?***" he demanded as he disappeared down the staircase.

He had put us meanwhile in the very chamber with the red curtains and the picture of Cupid and Psyche that Sitgreaves had described. Perhaps all the rooms were similarly decorated. I lounged on the bed while Sitgreaves sat on a chair and smoked....

I answered his last question, "No, they are true, but there is selection and form."

"While other memoirs have neither selection nor form and usually are not altogether accurate in the bargain...."

"Especially Madame Melba's...."

"Especially," agreed Sitgreaves delightedly, "Madame Melba's."

"Moore is really right," I went on. "He says that some people insist that Balzac was greater than Turgeniev, because the Frenchman took his characters from imagination, the Russian his from life. You will remember, however, that Edgar Saltus says, 'The manufacture of fiction from facts was begun by Balzac.' Moore's point is that all great writers write from observation. There is no other way. A character may have more or less resemblance to the original; it may be derived and bear a different name; still there must have been something.... In a letter which Moore once wrote me stands the phrase, 'Memory is the mother of the Muses.' 'Hail and Farewell' is just as much a work of imagination, according to Moore, as 'A Nest of Noblemen' or 'Les Illusions Perdues.'"

"Of course," admitted Sitgreaves. "No writer but what has suffered from the recognition of his characters. Dickens got into trouble.

Oscar Wilde is said to have done himself in 'Dorian Gray,' and Meredith's models for 'The Tragic Comedians' and 'Diana of the Crossways' are well known."

"All Moore has done is to call his characters by their real names and he has reported their conversations as he remembered them, but, mind you, he has not put into the book all their conversations, or even all the people he knew at that period. Arthur Symons, for instance, a great friend of Moore's at that time, is scarcely mentioned, and with reason: he has no part in the form of the book; its plot is not concerned with him.

"All artists create only in the image of the things they have seen, reduced to terms of art through their imagination. The paintings of Mina Loy seem to the beholder the strange creations of a vagrant fancy. I remember one picture of hers in which an Indian girl stands poised before an oriental palace, the most fantastic of palaces, it would seem. But the artist explained to me that it was simply the facade of Hagenbeck's menagerie in Hamburg, seen with an imaginative eye. The girl was a model.... One day on the beach at the Lido she saw a young man in a bathing suit lying stretched on the sand with his head in the lap of a beautiful woman. Other women surrounded the two. The group immediately suggested a composition to her. She went home and painted. She took the young man's bathing suit off and gave him wings; the women she dressed in lovely floating robes, and she called the picture, *l'Amour Dorlote par les Belles Dames*.

"And once I asked Frank Harris to explain to me the origin of his vivid story, 'Montes the Matador.' 'It's too simple,' he said, 'the model for Montes was a little Mexican greaser whom I met in Kansas. He was one of many in charge of cattle shipped up from Mexico and down from the States. All the white cattle men, the gringos, held him in great contempt. But,' continued Harris, speaking deliberately with his beautifully modulated voice, and his eyes twinkling with the memory of the thing, 'I soon found that the greaser's contempt for the gringos was immeasureably greater than their's for him. "Bah," he would say, "they know nothing." And it was so. He could go into a cattle car on a pitch dark night and make the bulls stand up, a feat that none of the white men would have attempted. I asked him how he did this and he told me the answer in three words, "I know them." He could go into a herd of cattle just let loose together and pick out their leader immediately, pick him out before the cattle themselves had! There was the origin of "Montes the Matador." He was named, of course, after the famous *torero* described by Gautier in his "Voyage en Espagne." When I was in Madrid sometime later I went to a number of bull-fights before I put the story together.' 'But,' I asked Harris, 'Is it possible for an *espada* to stand in the bull ring with his back to the bull, during a charge, as you have made him do frequently in the story?' 'Of course not,' he answered me at once, smiling his frankly malevolent smile, 'Of course not. That part was put in to show how much the public will stand for in a work of fiction. I believe one of the *espadas* tried it some time after the book appeared and was immediately killed.'

"Fiction, history, poetry, criticism, at their best, are all the same thing. When they inflame the imagination and stir the pulse they are identical: all creative work. It does not matter what a man writes about. It matters how he writes it. Subject is nothing. Should we regard Velasquez as less important than Murillo because the former painted portraits of contemporaries, whom in his fashion he criticized, while the Spanish Bouguereau disguised his models as the Virgin? Walter Pater's description of the *Monna Lisa* would live if the picture disappeared. Indeed it has created a factitious interest in da Vinci's masterwork. Even more might be said for Huysmans's description of Moreau's *Salome*, which actually puts the figures in the picture in motion! The critic, the historian at their best are creative artists as the writers of fiction are creative artists. Should we regard, for example, 'Imperial Purple' less a work of creative art than 'The Rise of Silas Lapham'?"

"I am getting your meaning more and more," said Sitgreaves. "And it occurs to me that perhaps I have been unjust in rating Moore low as a novelist. Perhaps I should have said that he is more successful in those books which depend more on his memory and less on his imaginative instinct. He cannot, after all, have known Jesus and Paul...."

"You are quite wrong," I said. "At least from his point of view. He says that he knows Paul better than he has ever known any one else. He even finds hair on Paul's chest. He can describe Paul, I believe, to the last mole. He knows his favourite colours, and whether he prefers artichokes to alligator pears. As for Christ, everybody professes to know Christ these days. Since the world has become distinctly un-Christian it has become comparatively easy to discuss Christ. He is regarded as an historical character, and a much more simple one than Napoleon. I have heard anarchists in bar-rooms talk about him by the hour, sometimes very graphically and always with a certain amount of wit. No, it is all the same.... Moore, now that he has been to Palestine and read the gospels, feels as well acquainted with Christ and Paul as he does with Edward Martyn and Yeats and Lady Gregory."

"I must fall back on the personal then," said Sitgreaves, now really at bay, "and say that I am less moved and interested when Moore is describing Evelyn Innes, than when he tells of his affair with Doris at Orelay."

"I am glad that you mentioned 'Evelyn Innes' again," I said, "because it is in this very book that he is said to have painted so many of his friends. Ulick Dean is undoubtedly Yeats. It has been suggested that

Arnold Dolmetsch posed for the portrait of Evelyn's father.
Dolmetsch's testimony on this point goes farther. He says that he
dictated certain passages in the book...."

"What is it, then? What is the difference? There is some difference,
of that I am sure...."

"The difference is--" I began when the door opened and Marcel entered,
the most amazingly comprehensive smile on his countenance.
"***Mademoiselle vous attend***," he said, and he looked the question.
"Shall I bring her in here?"

Sitgreaves answered it immediately, "***Je viens***." And then to me,
"Wait," as he vanished through the doorway.... I walked to the window,
drew aside the red curtains, and looked out into the fountain-splashed
court below....

* * * * *

"What is the difference?"

"I suppose it is that you prefer the new Moore to the old Moore, the
author of the later and better written books to the author of the
earlier ones. 'Evelyn Innes' was many times rewritten. Moore has said
that he could never get it to suit him, but he has also said,
recently, that he would never rewrite another book (a resolution he
has not kept). 'Memoirs of My Dead Life' and 'Hail and Farewell' do
not need rewriting. They are written to stand. 'The Brook Kerith,'
perhaps, you will find equally to your taste. It will be the newest
Moore...."

"You have explained to me," said Sitgreaves, "the difference: it is
one of development. Now that I think of it I don't believe that

Anatole France could write 'The Brook Kerith.'... It would be too symbolical, too cynical, in his hands. Moore will perhaps make it more human, by knowing the characters. I wonder," he continued musingly, as we left the room, and descended the stairs, "if he told you whether that hair on Paul's chest was red or black...."

February 1, 1915.

The Authoritative Work on
American Music

The Authoritative Work on American Music

H. L. Mencken pointed out to me recently, in his most earnest and persuasive manner, that it was my duty to write a book about the American composers, exposing their futile pretensions and describing their flaccid *opera*, stave by stave. It was in vain that I urged that this would be but a sleeveless errand, arguing that I could not fight men of straw, that these our composers had no real standing in the concert halls, and that pushing them over would be an easy exercise for a child of ten. On the contrary, he retorted, they belonged to the academies; certain people believed that they were important; it was necessary to dislodge this belief. I suggested, with a not too heavily assumed humility, that I had already done something of the sort in an essay entitled "The Great American Composer." "A good beginning," asserted Col. Mencken, "but not long enough. I won't

be satisfied with anything less than a book." "But if I wrote a book
about Professors Parker, Chadwick, Hadley, and the others I could find
nothing different to say about them; they are all alike. Neither
their lives nor their music offer opportunities for variations." "An
excellent idea!" cried Major Mencken, enthusiastically, "Write one
chapter and then repeat it verbatim throughout the book, changing only
the name of the principal character. Then clap on a preface,
explaining your reason for this procedure." My last protest was the
feeblest of all: "I can't spend a year or a month or a week poring
over the scores of these fellows; I can't go to concerts to hear their
music. I might as well go to work in a coal mine." "I'll do it for
you!" triumphantly checkmated General Mencken. "I'll read the scores
and you shall write the book!" And so he left me, as on a similar
occasion the fiend, having exhibited his prospectus, vanished from the
eyes of our Lord. And I returned to my home sorely troubled, finding
that the words of the man were running about in my head like so many
little Japanese waltzing mice.

And, after much cogitation, I went to such and such a book case and
took down a certain volume written by Louis Charles Elson (a very
large red tome) and another by Rupert Hughes, to see if their words of
praise for our weak musical brothers would stir me to action. I found
that they did not. My heart action remained normal; no film covered
my eyes; foam did not issue from my mouth. Indeed I read, quite
calmly, in Mr. Hughes's "American Composers" that A. J. Goodrich is
"recognized among scholars abroad as one of the leading spirits of our
time"; that "(Henry Holden) Huss has ransacked the piano and pillaged
almost every imaginable fabric of high colour.... The result is
gorgeous and purple"; that "The thing we are all waiting for is that
American grand opera, *The Woman of Marblehead* (by Louis Adolphe
Coerne). It is predicted that it will not receive the marble heart";
that "I know of no modern composer who has come nearer to relighting
the fires that burn in the old gavottes and fugues and preludes (than

Arthur Foote). His two gavottes are to me away the best since Bach";
that "the song (*Israfel* by Edgar Stillman-Kelley) is in my fervent
belief, a masterwork of absolute genius, one of the very greatest
lyrics in the world's music"; and in "The History of American Music"
by Louis C. Elson that "Music has made even more rapid strides than
literature among us," and that "he (George W. Chadwick) has reconciled
the symmetrical (sonata) form with modern passion." But it was in the
fourth volume of "The Art of Music," published by the National Society
of Music, that I found the supreme examples of this kind of writing.
The volume was edited by Arthur Farwell and W. Dermot Darby. Therein I
read with a sort of awed astonishment that one of the songs of
Frederick Ayres "reveals a poignancy of imagination and a perception
and apprehension of beauty seldom attained by any composer." I learned
that T. Carl Whitmer has a "spiritual kinship" with Arthur Shepherd,
Hans Pfitzner, and Vincent d'Indy. His music is "psychologically
subtle and spiritually rarefied: in colour it corresponds to the
violet end of the spectrum." I turned the pages until I came to the
name of Miss Gena Branscombe: "Inexhaustible buoyancy, a superlative
emotional wealth, and wholly singular gift of musical intuition are
the qualities which have shaped the composer's musical personality
(without much effort of the imagination we might say that they are the
qualities that shaped Beethoven's musical personality).... Her
impatient melodies leap and dash with youthful life, while her
accompaniments abound in harmonic hairbreadth escapes." Before he
became acquainted with the later French idiom Harvey W. Loomis
"spontaneously breathed forth the quality of spirit which we now
recognize in a Debussy or a Ravel."

Curiously enough, however, these statements did not annoy me. I found
no desire arising in me to deny them and doubtless, though mayhap with
a guilty conscience, I should have ditched the undertaking, consigned
it to that heap of undone duties, where already lie notes on a
comparison of Andalusian mules with the mules of Liane de Pougy, a few

scribbled memoranda for a treatise on the love habits of the mole, and a half-finished biography of the talented gentleman who signed his works, "Nick Carter," if my by this time quite roving eye had not alighted, entirely fortuitously, on one of the forgotten glories of my library, a slender volume entitled "Popular American Composers."

I recalled how I had bought this book. Happening into a modest second-hand bookshop on lower Third Avenue, maintained chiefly for the laudable purpose of redistributing paper novels of the Seaside and kindred libraries, of which, alas, we hear very little nowadays, I asked the proprietor if by chance he possessed any literature relating to the art of music. By way of answer, he retired to the very back of his little room, searched for a space in a litter on the floor, and then returned with a pile of nine volumes or so in his arms. The titles, such as "Great Violinists," "Harmony in Thirteen Lessons," and "How to Sing," did not intrigue me, but in idly turning the pages of this "Popular American Composers" I came across a half-tone reproduction of a photograph of Paul Dresser, the only less celebrated brother of Theodore Dreiser, with a short biography of the composer of *On the Banks of the Wabash*. As Sir George Grove in his excellent dictionary neglected to mention this portentous name in American Art and Letters (although he devoted sixty-seven pages, printed in double columns, to Mendelssohn) I saw the advantage of adding the little book to my collection. The bookseller, when questioned, offered to relinquish the volume for a total of fifteen cents, and I carried it away with me. Once I had become more thoroughly acquainted with its pages I realized that I would willingly have paid fifteen dollars for it.

This book, indeed, cannot fail to delight General Mencken. There is no reference in its pages to Edgar Stillman-Kelley, Miss Gena Branscombe, Louis Adolphe Coerne, Henry Holden Huss, T. Carl Whitmer, Arthur Farwell, Arthur Foote, or A. J. Goodrich. In fact, if we overlook brief notices of John Philip Sousa, Harry von Tilzer, Paul Dresser, Charles K. Harris, and Hattie Starr (whom you will immediately recall as the composer of **Little Alabama Coon**), the author, Frank L. Boyden, has not hesitated to go to the roots of his subject, pushing aside the college professors and their dictums, and has turned his attention to figures in the art life of America, from whom, Mencken himself, I feel sure, would not take a single paragraph of praise, so richly is it deserved. I am unfamiliar with the causes contributing to this book's comparative obscurity; perhaps, indeed, they are similar to those responsible for the early failure of "Sister Carrie." May not we even suspect that the odium cast by the Doubledays on the author of that romance might have been actively transferred in some degree to a work which contained a biographical notice and a picture of his brother? At any rate, "Popular American Composers," published in 1902, fell into undeserved oblivion and so I make no apology for inviting my readers to peruse its pages with me.

Opening the book, then, at random, I discover on page 96 a biography of Lottie A. Kellow (her photograph graces the reverse of this page). In a few well-chosen words (almost indeed in "gipsy phrases") Mr. Boyden gives us the salient details of her career. Mrs. Kellow is a resident of Cresco, Iowa, a church singer of note, and the possessor of a contralto voice of great volume. As a composer she has to her credit "marches, cakewalks, schottisches, and other styles of instrumental music." We are given a picture of Mrs. Kellow at work: "Mrs. Kellow's best efforts are made in the evening, and in darkness, save the light of the moonbeams on the keys of her piano." We are also told that "she is happy in her inspirations and a sincere lover of music. All of her compositions show a decided talent and possess musical elements which are only to be found in the works of an artist. Mrs. Kellow's musical friends are confident of her success as a composer and predict for her a brilliant future."

Let us turn to the somewhat more extensive biography of W. T. Mullin on Page 4 (his photograph faces this page). Almost in the first line the author rewards our attention: "To him may be applied the simplest and grandest eulogy Shakespeare ever pronounced: 'He was a man.'" We are also informed that he was born of a cultured family, that his inherited nobility of character has been carefully fostered by a thorough education, and told that one finds in him the unusual combination of genius wedded to sound common sense and practical business capacity. His family moved to Colorado, Texas, while he was still a lad and here his musical talent began to display itself. "The inventive faculties of the small boy, and the innate harmony of the musician, combined to improvise a crude instrument which emitted the notes of the scale. Successful at drawing forth a concord of sweet sounds, he continued to experiment upon everything which would emit musical vibrations. (Even the pigs, I take it, did not escape.) He consequently discovered the laws of vibrating chords before he had mastered the intricacies of the multiplication table. Yet strange as it may seem, his musical education was neglected. A four months' course in piano instruction was interrupted and then resumed for two months more. Upon this meagre foundation rested his subsequent phenomenal progress." I pause to point out to the astonished and breathless reader that even Mozart and Schubert, infant prodigies that they were, received more training than this.

I continue to quote: "At the age of thirteen he joined The Colorado (Texas) Cornet Band as a charter member. The youngest member of the band, he soon outstripped his comrades by virtue of his superior natural ability. His position was that of second tenor. Wearying of the monotony of playing, he determined to venture on solo work. The boy felt the impetus of restless power and the following incident illustrates his remarkable originality. Taking the piano score of a favourite melody he transposed it within the compass of the second tenor. This feat evoked admiring applause because of his extreme youth and untrained abilities. The band-master remarked that elderly and experienced heads could hardly have accomplished this.

"From boyhood to manhood he has remained with the Colorado (Texas) band as one of its most efficient members, composing in his leisure moments, marches, ragtimes, waltzes, song and dance schottisches, etc. Of his many meritorious compositions only one has so far been given to the public:-- ***The West Texas Fair March***, composed for and dedicated to the management of the West Texas Fair and Round-up. This institution holds its annual meetings at Abilene, Texas. There the march was played for the first time at their October, 1899, meet with great success, and again at their September, 1900, meet by the Stockman band of Colorado, Texas, which has furnished music for the West Texas Fair during their 1899 and 1900 meetings. Mr. Mullin's position in the Stockman band is that of euphonium soloist. He is a proficient performer upon all band instruments from cornet to tuba, including slide trombone, his favourites being the baritone and the trombone.

"He plays many stringed instruments, as well as the piano and organ. He is the proud possessor of a genuine Stradivarius violin--a family heirloom--which he naturally prizes beyond the intrinsic value. The feat of playing on several instruments at once presents no difficulty to him.

"This briefly sketches Mr. Mullin's life, character and ability as a musician. His accompanying photograph reveals his superb physique. Personally he possesses charming, agreeable manners and Chesterfieldan courteousness, which vastly contributes to his popularity. Sincere devotion to his art has been rewarded by that elevating nobility of soul, which alone can penetrate the blue expanse of space and revel in the music of the spheres."

What more is there to say? I can only assure the reader that Mullin stands unique among all musicians, creative and interpretative, in being able to play the organ, many stringed instruments, and all the instruments in a brass band (several of them simultaneously; it would be interesting to know which and how) after studying the piano for six months. I sincerely hope that the mistake he made in withholding all his compositions, save one, from the public, has been rectified.

Helen Kelsey Fox, like so many of our talented men and women, has a European strain in her blood. She is a lineal descendant on her mother's side of a French nobleman and a German princess. Nevertheless she continues to reside in Vermilion, Ohio. She is of a "decided poetic nature and lives in an atmosphere of her own. She dwells in a world of thought peopled by the creations of an active and lyric mentality." She is so imbued with the poetic spark that, as she expresses it, she "speaks in rhyme half the time."

John Z. Macdonald, strictly speaking, is not an American composer. He was born in Scotland and came to America in 1881 at the age of 21, but as he is one of the very few composers since Nero to enter public political life he well deserves a place in this collection. In 1890 he was elected city clerk of Brazil, Indiana, a position which he held for seven years. In 1898 he was elected treasurer of Clay County, Indiana. This county is democratic "by between five and six hundred" but Mr. Macdonald was elected on the republican ticket by a majority of 133. He was the only republican elected. Among the best known of Mr. Macdonald's compositions is his famous "expansion" song, in which he predicted the fate of Aguinaldo. He has autograph letters, praising this song, from the late President McKinley, Col. Roosevelt, General Harrison, Admiral Schley, John Philip Sousa and other "eminent gentlemen."

Edward Dyer, born in Washington, was the son of a marble cutter who "helped to erect the U. S. Treasury, Patent Office, and Capitol.... In the majority of his compositions there is a tinge of sadness which appeals to his auditors.... Mr. Dyer never descends to coarseness or vulgarity in his productions; he writes pure, clean words, something that can be sung in the home, school and on the stage to refined respectable people."

We learn much of the study years of Mrs. Lucy L. Taggart: "From earliest childhood she received valuable musical instruction from her father (Mr. Longsdon) who, coming from England in 1835, purchased the first piano that came to Chicago, an elegant hand-carved instrument that is still treasured in the old home." Later "she studied under Prof. C. E. Brown, of Owego, N. Y., Prof. Heimburger, of San Francisco and Herr Chas. Goffrie. Mrs. Taggart was also for five years a pupil of Senor Arevalo, the famous guitar soloist of Los Angeles.... Mrs. Taggart has in preparation (1902) **Methought He Touched the Strings**, an idyl for piano in memory of the late Senor M. S. Arevalo."

David Weidley, born in Philadelphia, is the composer of the following songs, **Old Spooney Spooppalay**, **Jennie Ree**, **Autumn Leaves**, **Hannah Glue**, and **Uncle Reuben and Aunt Lucinda**. "He has done much to create and elevate a taste for music in the community where he resides and where he is known as 'Dave.' Even the little children call him 'Dave' as freely and innocently as those who have known him for years, and there can be no greater compliment for any man than that he is known and loved by the children. Mr. Weidley is by profession a sheet metal worker. He is a P. G. of the I. O. O. F., and a P. C. in the Knights of Pythias. He is not identified with any church, but loves and serves his fellow-men."

In the biography of Delmer G. Palmer we are assured that "Versatility is a trait with which musical composers are not excessively burdened. There are few performers who can include **The Moonlight Sonata** and

Schubert's **Serenade** with selections from **The Merry-go-round**, and do justice to the expression of each, much less would such adaptability be looked for among composers. As most rules have exceptions, in this there is one who stands in a class occupied by no one else, Mr. Delmer G. Palmer, the 'Green Mountain Composer,' who at present resides in Kansas City.

"As recently as 1899 Mr. Palmer wrote a song in the popular 'ragtime,' **My Sweetheart is a Midnight Coon** and almost in the same breath also wrote the heavy sacred solo, **Christ in Gethsemane**. The first is of the usual light order characteristic of this class of music. The latter is as far removed to the contrary as is comedy from tragedy. The 'coon' song entered the bubbling effervescing cauldron of what is termed 'ragtime' music among the multitudinous others, and soon was seen peeping through at the surface among the lightest and most catchy.... The sacred solo found its level among the heavier in its class, and if the term may be here applied, it was also a hit."

S. Duncan Baker, born August 25, 1855, still lives (1902) in the old family residence at Natchez, Miss. "In this house is located the den where he has spent many hours with his collection of banjos and pictures and in writing for and playing on the instrument which he adopted as a favourite during its dark days (about 1871)." We are told that he composed an "artistic banjo solo," entitled, Memories of Farland. *"Had this production or its companion piece,* Thoughts of the Cadenza, been written by an old master for some other instrument and later have been adapted by a modern composer to the banjo, either or both of them would have been pronounced classic, barring some slight defects in form."

I cannot stop to quote from the delightful accounts offered us of the lives and works of Albert Matson, George D. Tufts, D. O. Loy, Lavinia Pascoe Oblad, and forty or fifty other American singers, but it seems to me that I have done enough, Mencken, to prove to you that the great book on American music has been written. Without one single mention of the names of Horatio Parker, George W. Chadwick, Frederick Converse, or Henry Hadley, by a transference of the emphasis to the place where it belongs, the author of this undying book has answered your prayer.

December 11, 1917.

Old Days and New

Old Days and New

Some toothless old sentimentalist or other periodically sets up a melancholy howl for "the good old days of comic opera," whatever or whenever they were. Perhaps none of us, once past forty, is guiltless in this respect. Nothing, not even the smell of an apple-blossom from the old homestead, the sight of a daguerreotype of a miss one kissed at the age of ten, or a taste of a piece of the kind of pie that "mother used to make" so arouses the sensibility of a man of middle age as the memory of some musical show which he saw in his budding manhood. That is why revivals of these venerable institutions are frequently projected and, some of them, very successfully accomplished. When a manager revives an old drama he must appeal to the interest of his audience; it may not be the identical interest which held the original spectators of the piece spell-bound, but, none the less, it must be an interest. When a manager revives an old musical comedy he appeals directly to sentiment.

Of course, the exact date of the good old days is a variable quantity. I have known a vain regretter to turn no further back than to the nights of ***The Merry Widow***, ***The Waltz Dream***, The Chocolate Soldier, The Girl in the Train, ***and*** The Dollar Princess, in other words to the Viennese renaissance; another, in using the phrase, is subconsciously conjuring up pictures of ***La Belle Helene***, Orphee aux Enfers, ***or*** La Fille de Madame Angot, good fodder for memory to feed on here; a third will instinctively revert to the Johann Strauss operetta period, the era of ***The Queen's Lace Handkerchief*** and Die Fledermaus; a fourth cries, "Give us Gilbert and Sullivan!" A fifth, when his ideas are chased to their lair, will rhapsodize endlessly over the charms of the London Gaiety when ***The Geisha***, The Country Girl, ***and*** The Circus Girl were in favour; a sixth, it seems, finds his pleasure in Americana, ***Robin Hood***, ***Wang***, The Babes in Toyland, ***and*** El Capitan; a seventh becomes maudlin to the most utter degree when you mention ***Les Cloches de Corneville***, or La Mascotte, products of a decadent stage in the history of French opera-bouffe. Not long ago I heard a man speak of the cadet operas in Boston (did a man named Barnet write them?) as the last of the great musical pieces; and every one of you who reads this essay will have a brother, or a son, or a friend who went to see ***Sybil*** forty-three times and ***The Girl from Utah*** seventy-six. Twenty years from now, as he sits before the open fire, the mere mention of They Wouldn't Believe Me will cause the tears to course down his cheeks as he pats the pate of his infant son or daughter and weepingly describes the never-to-be-forgotten fascination of Julia Sanderson, the (in the then days) unattainable agility of Donald Brian.

In no other form of theatrical entertainment is the appeal to softness so direct. The man who attends a performance of a musical farce goes in a good mood, usually with a couple of friends, or possibly with *the* girl. If he has dined well and his digestion is in working order and he is young enough, the spell of the lights and the music is irresistible to his receptive and impressionable nature. There are those young men, of course, who are constant attendants because of the altogether too wonderful hair of the third girl from the right in the front row. Others succumb to the dental perfection of the prima donna or to the shapely legs of the soubrette. All of us, I am almost proud to admit, at some time or other, are subject to the contagion. I well remember the year in which I considered myself as a possible suitor for the hand of Della Fox. Photographs and posters of this deity adorned my walls. I was an assiduous collector of newspaper clippings referring to her profoundly interesting activities, although my sophistication had not reached the stage where I might appeal to Romeike for assistance. The mere mention of Miss Fox's name was sufficient cause to make me blush profusely. Eventually my father was forced to take steps in the matter when I began, in a valiant effort to summon up the spirit of the lady's presence, to disturb the early morning air with vocal assaults on **She Was a Daisy**, which, you will surely remember, was the musical gem of **The Little Trooper**. Here are the words of the refrain:

> "She was a daisy, daisy, daisy!
> Driving me crazy, crazy, crazy!
> Helen of Troy and Venus were to her cross-eyed crones!
> She was dimpled and rosy, rosy, rosy!
> Sweet as a posy, posy, posy!
> How I doted upon her, my Ann Jane Jones!"

You will admit, I think, at first glance, the superior literary quality of these lines; you will perceive at once to what immeasurably higher class of art they belong than the lyrics that librettists forge for us today.

Wall Street broker, poet, green grocer, soldier, banker, lawyer, whatever you are, confess the facts to yourself: you were once as I. You have suffered the same feelings that I suffered. Perhaps with you it was not Della Fox.... Who then? Did saucy Marie Jansen awaken your admiration? Was pert Lulu Glaser the object of your secret but persistent attention? How many times did you go to see Marie Tempest in *The Fencing Master*, or Alice Nielsen in *The Serenade*? Was Virginia Earle in *The Circus Girl* the idol of your youth or was it Mabel Barrison in *The Babes in Toyland*? Theresa Vaughn in *1492*, May Yohe in *The Lady Slavey*, Hilda Hollins in *The Magic Kiss*, or Nancy McIntosh in *His Excellency*? Madge Lessing in Jack and the Beanstalk, *Edna May in* The Belle of New York, Phyllis Rankin in *The Rounders*, or Gertrude Quinlan in *King Dodo*?

What do you whistle in your bathtub when you are in a reminiscent mood? Is it *The Typical Tune of Zanzibar*, or Baby, Baby, Dance My Darling Baby, *or* Starlight, Starbright, *or* Tell Me, Pretty Maiden, *or* A Simple Little String, *or* J'aime les Militaires (if you whistle this, ten to one your next door neighbour thinks you have been to an orchestra concert and heard Beethoven's Seventh Symphony), or *Sister Mary Jane's Top Note*, or A Wandering Minstrel I, *or* See How It Sparkles, *or the* Lullaby from *Erminie*, which Pauline Hall used to sing as if she herself were asleep, and which Emma Abbott interpolated in *The Mikado*, or A Pretty Girl, A Summer Night, *or the* Policeman's Chorus *from* The Pirates of Penzance, *or* The Soldiers in the Park, *or* My Angeline, or the *Letter Song* from *The Chocolate Soldier*, or I'm Little Buttercup, *or the* Gobble Song *from* The Mascot, *or the* Anna Song from *Nanon*, or the march from *Fatinitza*, or I'm All the Way from Gay Paree, *or* Love Comes Like a Summer Sigh, *or* In the North Sea

Lived a Whale, *or* Jusqu'la, *or* The Harmless Little Girlie With the Downcast Eyes, *or* They All Follow Me, *or* The Amorous Goldfish, or ***Don't Be Cross***, or ***Slumber On, My Little Gypsy Sweetheart***, or ***Good-bye Flo***, or ***La Legende de la Mere Angot***, or ***My Alamo Love***?

There is a very subtle and fragrant charm about these old recollections which the sight or sound of a score, a view of an old photograph of Lillian Russell or Judic, or a dip in the Theatre Complet of Meilhac and Halevy will reawaken. But it is only at a revival of one of our old favourites that we can really bathe in sentimentality, drink in draughts of joy from the past, allow memory full away. You whose hair is turning white will be in Row A, Seat No. 1 for the first performance of a revival of ***Robin Hood***. You will not hear Edwin Hoff in his original role; Jessie Bartlett Davis is dead and, alas, Henry Clay Barnabee is no longer on the boards, but the newcomers, possibly, are respectable substitutes and the airs and lines remain. You can walk about in the lobby and say proudly that you attended the *first* performance of the opera ever so long ago when operettas had tune and reason. "Yes sir, there were plots in those days, and composers, and the singers could *act*. Times have certainly changed, sir. Come to the corner and have a Manhattan.... There were no cocktails in those days.... There is no singer like Mrs. Davis today!"

Well the poor souls who cannot feel tenderly about a past they have not yet experienced have their recompenses. For one thing I am certain that the revivals of the Gilbert and Sullivan operettas to which De Wolf Hopper devoted his best talents were better, in many respects, than the original London productions; just as I am equally certain that the representations of ***Aida*** at the Metropolitan Opera House are way ahead of the original performance of that work given at Cairo before the Khedive of Egypt.

Then there is the musical revue, a form which we have borrowed from the French, but which we have vastly improved upon and into which we have poured some of our most national feeling and expression. The interpretation of these frivolities is a new art. Gaby Deslys may be only half a loaf compared to Marie Jansen, but I am sure that Elsie Janis is more than three-quarters. Frank Tinney and Al Jolson can, in their humble way, efface memories of Digby Bell and Dan Daly. Adele Rowland and Marie Dressler have their points (and curves). Irving Berlin, Louis A. Hirsch, and Jerome Kern are not to be sniffed at. Neither is P. G. Wodehouse. Harry B. Smith we have always with us: he is the Sarah Bernhardt of librettists.

Joseph Urban has wrought a revolution in stage settings for this form of entertainment. Louis Sherwin has offered us convincing evidence to support his theory that the new staging in America is coming to us by way of the revue and not through the serious drama. Melville Ellis, Lady Duff-Gordon, and Paul Poiret have done their bit for the dresses. In fact, my dear young man--who are reading this article--you will feel just as tenderly in twenty years about the *Follies of 1917* as your father does now about *Wang*. Only, and this is a very big ONLY, the *Follies of 1917*, depending as it does entirely on topical subjects and dimpled knees, cannot be revived. Fervid and enlivening as its immediate impression may be it cannot be lasting. You can never recapture the thrills of this summer by sitting in Row A, Seat No. 1 at any 1937 *reprise*. There can never be anything of the sort. The revue, like the firefly, is for a night only. We take it in with the daily papers ... and the next season, already old-fashioned, it goes forth to show Grinnell and Davenport how Mlle. Manhattan deported herself the year before.

So if the youth of these days chooses to be sentimental in the years to come over the good old days of Urban scenery and Olive Thomas, the Balloon Girls of the Midnight Frolic and the chorus of the Winter

Garden, he will be obliged to give way to the mood at home in front of the fire, see the pictures in the smoke, and hear the tunes in the dropping of the coals. Which is perhaps as it should be. For in 1937 the youth of that epoch can sit in Row A, Seat No. 1 himself and not be ousted from his place by a sentimental gentleman of middle age who longs to hear *Poor Butterfly* again.

April 25, 1917.

Two Young American Playwrights

"Gautier had a theory to the effect that to be a member of the Academy was simply and solely a matter of predestination. 'There is no need to do anything,' he would say, 'and so far as the writing of books is concerned that is entirely useless. A man is born an Academician as he is born a bishop or a cook. He can abuse the Academy in a dozen pamphlets if it amuses him, and be elected all the same; but if he is not predestined, three hundred volumes and ten masterpieces, recognized as such by the genuflections of an adoring universe, will not aid him to open its doors.' Evidently Balzac was not predestined but then neither was Moliere, and there must have been some consolation for him in that."

Edgar Saltus.

Two Young American Playwrights

In the newspaper reports relating to the death of Auguste Rodin I read with some astonishment that if the venerable sculptor, who lacked three years of being eighty when he died, had lived two weeks longer he would have been admitted to the French Academy! In other words, the greatest stone-poet since Michael Angelo, internationally famous and powerful, the most striking artist figure, indeed, of the last half century, was to be permitted, in the extremity of old age, to inscribe his name on a scroll, which bore the signatures of many inoffensive nobodies. I could not have been more amused if the newspapers, in publishing the obituary notices of John Jacob Astor, had announced that if the millionaire had not perished in the sinking of the *Titanic*, his chances of being invited to join the Elks were good; or if "Variety" or some other tradespaper of the music halls, had proclaimed, just before Sarah Bernhardt's debut at the Palace Theatre, that if her appearances there were successful she might expect an invitation to membership in the White Rats.... These hypothetical instances would seem ridiculous ... but they are not. The Rodin case puts a by no means seldom-recurring phenomenon in the centre of the stage under a calcium light. The ironclad dreadnaughts of the academic world, the reactionary artists, the dry-as-dust lecturers are constantly ignoring the most vital, the most real, the most important artists while they sing polyphonic, antiphonal, Palestrinian motets in praise of men who have learned to imitate comfortably and efficiently the work of their predecessors.

     *   *   *   *   *

If there are other contemporary French sculptors than Rodin their names elude me at the moment; yet I have no doubt that some ten or fifteen of these hackmen have their names emblazoned in the books of all the so-called "honour" societies in Paris. It is a comfort, on the whole, to realize that America is not the only country in which such things happen. As a matter of fact, they happen nowhere more often than in France.

If some one should ask you suddenly for a list of the important playwrights of France today, what names would you let roll off your tongue, primed by the best punditic and docile French critics? Henry Bataille, Paul Hervieu, and Henry Bernstein. Possibly Rostand. Don't deny this; you know it is true, unless it happens you have been doing some thinking for yourself. For even in the works of Remy de Gourmont (to be sure this very clairvoyant mind did not often occupy itself with dramatic literature) you will find little or nothing relating to Octave Mirbeau and Georges Feydeau. True, Mirbeau did not do his best work in the theatre. That stinging, cynical attack on the courts of Justice (?) of France (nay, the world!), "Le Jardin de Supplice" is not a play and it is probably Mirbeau's masterpiece and the best piece of critical fiction written in France (or anywhere else) in the last fifty years. However Mirbeau shook the pillars of society even in the playhouse. *Le Foyer* was hissed repeatedly at the Theatre Francais. Night after night the proceedings ended in the ejection and arrest of forty or fifty spectators. Even to a mere outsider, an idle bystander of the boulevards, this complete exposure of the social, moral, and political hypocricies of a nation seemed exceptionally brutal. Le Foyer and "Le Jardin" could only have been written by a man passionately devoted to the human ideal ("each as she may," as Gertrude Stein so beautifully puts it). Les Affaires sont les Affaires is pure theatre, perhaps, but it might be considered the best play produced in France between Becque's *La Parisienne* and Brieux's *Les Hannetons*.

It is not surprising, on the whole, to find the critical tribe turning for relief from this somewhat unpleasant display of Gallic closet skeletons to the discreet exhibition of a few carefully chosen bones in the plays of Bernstein and Bataille, direct descendants of Scribe, Sardou, *et Cie*, but I may be permitted to indulge in a slight snicker of polite amazement when I discover these gentlemen applying their fingers to their noses in no very pretty-meaning gesture, directed at a grandson of Moliere. For such is Georges Feydeau. His method is not that of the Seventeenth Century master, nor yet that of Mirbeau; nevertheless, aside from these two figures, Beaumarchais, Marivaux, Becque, Brieux at his best, and Maurice Donnay occasionally, there has not been a single writer in the history of the French theatre so inevitably *au courant* with human nature. His form is frankly farcical and his plays are so funny, so enjoyable merely as *good shows* that it seems a pity to raise an obelisk in the playwright's honour, and yet the fact remains that he understands the political, social, domestic, amorous, even cloacal conditions of the French better than any of his contemporaries, always excepting the aforementioned Mirbeau. In *On Purge Bebe* he has written saucy variations on a theme which Rabelais, Boccaccio, George Moore, and Moliere in collaboration would have found difficult to handle. It is as successful an experiment in bravado and bravura as Mr. Henry James's "The Turn of the Screw." And he has accomplished this feat with nimbleness, variety, authority, even (granting the subject) delicacy. Seeing it for the first time you will be so submerged in gales of uncontrollable laughter that you will perhaps not recognize at once how every line reveals character, how every situation springs from the foibles of human nature. Indeed in this one-act farce Feydeau, with about as much trouble as Zeus took in transforming his godship into the semblance of a swan, has given you a well-rounded picture of middle-class life in France with its external and internal implications.... And how he understands the buoyant French *grue*, unselfconscious and undismayed in any situation. I sometimes think that *Occupe-toi d'Amelie* is the most satisfactory play I have ever

seen; it is certainly the most delightful. I do not think you can see
it in Paris again. The Nouveautes, where it was presented for over a
year, has been torn down; an English translation would be an insult
to Feydeau; nor will you find essays about it in the yellow volumes in
which the French critics tenderly embalm their **feuilletons**; nor do I
think Arthur Symons or George Moore, those indefatigable diggers in
Parisian graveyards, have discovered it for their English readers.
Reading the play is to miss half its pleasure; so you must take my
word in the matter unless you have been lucky enough to see it
yourself, in which case ten to one you will agree with me that one
such play is worth a kettleful of boiled-over drama like **Le Voleur**,
Le Secret, **Samson**, **La Vierge Folle**, **et cetera**, **et cetera**. In
the pieces I have mentioned Feydeau, in representation, had the
priceless assistance of a great comic artist, Armande Cassive. If we
are to take Mr. Symons's assurance in regard to de Pachmann that he is
the world's greatest pianist because he does one thing more perfectly
than any one else, by a train of similar reasoning we might
confidently assert that Mlle. Cassive is the world's greatest actress.

When you ask a Frenchman to explain why he does not like Mirbeau (and
you will find that Frenchmen invariably do not like him) he will shrug
his shoulders and begin to tell you that Mirbeau was not good to his
mother, or that he drank to excess, or that he did not wear a red,
white, and blue coat on the Fourteenth of July, or that he did not
stand for the French spirit as exemplified in the eating of snails on
Christmas. In other words, he will immediately place himself in a
position in which you may be excused for regarding him as a person
whose opinion is worth nothing, whereas his ratiocinatory powers on
subjects with which he is more in sympathy may be excellent. I know
why he does not like Mirbeau. Mirbeau is the reason. In his life he
was not accustomed to making compromises nor was he accustomed to
making friends (which comes after all to the same thing). He did what
he pleased, said what he pleased, wrote what he pleased. His armorial

bearings might have been a cat upsetting a cream jug with the motto, "*Je m'en fous*." The author of "Le Jardin de Supplice" would not be in high favour anywhere; nevertheless I would willingly relinquish any claims I might have to future popularity for the privilege of having been permitted to sign this book.

Feydeau is distinctly another story; his plays are more successful than any others given in Paris. They are so amusing that even while he is pointing the finger at your own particular method of living you are laughing so hard that you haven't time to see the application.... So the French critics have set him down as another popular figure, only a nobody born to entertain the boulevards, just as the American critics regard the performances of Irving Berlin with a steely supercilious impervious eye. The Viennese scorned Mozart because he entertained them. "A gay population," wrote the late John F. Runciman, "always a heartless master, holds none in such contempt as the servants who provide it with amusement."

The same condition has prevailed in England until recently. A few seasons ago you might have found the critics pouring out their glad songs about Arthur Wing Pinero and Henry Arthur Jones. Bernard Shaw has, in a measure, restored the balance to the British theatre. He is not only a brilliant playwright; he is a brilliant critic as well. Foreseeing the fate of the under man in such a struggle he became his own literary huckster and by outcriticizing the other critics he easily established himself as the first English (or Irish) playwright. When he thus rose to the top, by dint of his own exertions, he had strength enough to carry along with him a number of other important authors. As a consequence we may regard the Pinero incident closed and in ten years his theatre will be considered as old-fashioned and as inadept as that of Robertson or Bulwer-Lytton.

Having no Shaw in America, no man who can write brilliant prefaces and essays about his own plays until the man in the street is obliged perforce to regard them as literature, we find ourselves in the condition of benighted France. Dulness is mistaken for literary flavour; the injection of a little learning, of a little poetry (so-called) into a theatrical hackpiece, is the signal for a good deal of enthusiasm on the part of the journalists (there are two brilliant exceptions). Which of our playwrights are taken seriously by the pundits? Augustus Thomas and Percy MacKaye: Thomas the dean, and MacKaye the poet laureate. I have no intention of wrenching the laurel wreathes from these august brows. Let them remain. Each of these gentlemen has a long and honourable career in the theatre behind him, from which he should be allowed to reap what financial and honourary rewards he may be able. But I would not add one leaf to these wreathes, nor one crotchet to the songs of praise which vibrate around them. I turn aside from their plays in the theatre and in the library as I turn aside from the fictions of Pierre de Coulevain and Arnold Bennett.

I love to fashion wreathes of my own and if two young men will now step forward to the lecturer's bench I will take delight in crowning them with my own hands. Will the young man at the back of the hall please page Avery Hopwood and Philip Moeller?... No response! They seem to have retreated modestly into the night. Nevertheless they shall not escape me!

I speak of Mr. Hopwood first because he has been writing for our theatre for a longer period than has Mr. Moeller, and because his position, such as it is, is assured. Like Feydeau in France he has a large popular following; he has probably made more money in a few years than Mr. Thomas has made during his whole lifetime and the managers are always after him to furnish them with more plays with which to fill their theatres. For his plays do fill the theatres. *Fair and Warmer*, *Nobody's Widow*, *Clothes*, and *Seven Days*, would be included in any list of the successful pieces produced in New York within the past ten years. Two of these pieces would be near the very top of such a list. An utterly absurd allotment of actors is sufficient to explain the failures of **Sadie Love** and Our Little Wife and it might be well if some one should attempt a revival of one of his three serious plays, **This Woman and This Man**, in which Carlotta Nillson appeared for a brief space.

This author, mainly through the beneficent offices of a gift of supernal charm, contrives to do in English very much what Feydeau does in French. It is his contention that you can smite the Puritans, even in the American theatre, squarely on the cheek, provided you are sagacious in your choice of weapon. In **Fair and Warmer** he provokes the most boisterous and at the same time the most innocent laughter with a scene which might have been made insupportably vulgar. A perfectly respectable young married woman gets very drunk with the equally respectable husband of one of her friends. The scene is the mainstay, the **raison d'etre**, of the play, and it furnishes the material for the better part of one act; yet young and old, rich and poor, philistine and superman alike, delight in it. To make such a situation irresistible and universal in its appeal is, it seems to me, undoubtedly the work of genius. What might, indeed should, have been disgusting, was not only in intention but in performance very funny. Let those who do not appreciate the virtuosity of this undertaking attempt to write as successful a scene in a similar vein. Even if they are able to do so, and I do not for a moment believe that there is another dramatic author in America who can, they will be the first to grant the difficulty of the achievement. With an apparently inexhaustible fund of fantasy and wit Mr. Hopwood passes his wand over certain phases of so-called smart life, almost always with the happiest results. With a complete realization of the independence of his medium he often ignores the realistic conventions and the traditional technique of the stage, but his touch is so light and joyous, his wit so free from pose, that he rarely fails to establish his effect. His pen has seldom faltered. Occasionally, however, the heavy hand of an uncomprehending stage director or of an aggressive actor has played havoc with the delicate texture of his fabric. There is no need here for the use of hammer or trowel; if an actress must seek aid in implements, let her rather rely on a soft brush, a lacy handkerchief, or a sparkling spangled fan.

Philip Moeller has achieved distinction in another field, that of elegant burlesque, of sublimated caricature. His stage men and women are as adroitly distorted (the better to expose their comic possibilities) as the drawings of Max Beerbohm. Beginning with the Bible and the Odyssey (*Helena's Husband* and *Sisters of Susannah* for the Washington Square Players) he has at length, by way of Shakespeare and Bacon (*The Roadhouse in Arden*) arrived at the Romantic Period in French literature and in *Madame Sand*, his first three-act play, he has established himself at once as a dangerous rival of the authors of *Caesar and Cleopatra* and The Importance of Being Earnest, *both plays in the same* genre as Mr. Moeller's latest contribution to the stage. The author has thrown a very high light on the sentimental adventures of the writing lady of the early Nineteenth Century, has indeed advised us and convinced us that they were somewhat ridiculous. So they must have appeared even to her contemporaries, however seriously George took herself, her romances, her passions, her petty tragedies. A less adult, a less seriously trained mind might have fallen into the error of making a sentimental play out of George's affairs with Alfred de Musset, Dr. Pagello, and Chopin (Mr. Moeller contents himself with these three passions, selected from the somewhat more extensive list offered to us by history). Such an author would doubtless have written Great Catherine *in the style of* Disraeli *and* Androcles and the Lion after the manner of *Ben Hur*! Whether love itself is always a comic subject, as Bernard Shaw would have us believe, is a matter for dispute, but there can be no alternative opinion about the loves of George Sand. A rehearsal of them offers only laughter to any one but a sentimental school girl.

The piece is conceived on a true literary level; it abounds in wit, in fantasy, in delightful situations, but there is nothing precious about its progress. Mr. Moeller has carefully avoided the traps expressly laid for writers of such plays. For example, the enjoyment of Madame Sand is in no way dependent upon a knowledge of the books of that authoress, De Musset, and Heine, nor yet upon an acquaintance with the music of Liszt and Chopin. Such matters are pleasantly and lightly referred to when they seem pertinent, but no insistence is laid upon them. Occasionally our author has appropriated some phrase originally spoken or written by one of the real characters, but for that he can scarcely be blamed. Indeed, when one takes into consideration the wealth of such material which lay in books waiting for him, it is surprising that he did not take more advantage of it. In the main he has relied on his own cleverness to delight our ears for two hours with brilliant conversation.

There is, it should be noted, in conclusion, nothing essentially American about either of these young authors. Both Mr. Hopwood and Mr. Moeller might have written for the foreign stage. Several of Mr. Hopwood's pieces, indeed, have already been transported to foreign climes and there seems every reason for belief that Mr. Moeller's comedy will meet a similarly happy fate.

November 29, 1917.

De Senectute Cantorum

"All'eta di settanta
Non si ama, ne si canta."

Italian proverb.

De Senectute Cantorum

"I am not sure," writes Arthur Symons in his admirable essay on Sarah Bernhardt, "that the best moment to study an artist is not the moment of what is called decadence. The first energy of inspiration is gone; what remains is the method, the mechanism, and it is that which alone one can study, as one can study the mechanism of the body, not the principle of life itself. What is done mechanically, after the heat of the blood has cooled, and the divine accidents have ceased to happen, is precisely all that was consciously skilful in the performance of an art. To see all this mechanism left bare, as the form of a skeleton is left bare when age thins the flesh upon it is to learn more easily all that is to be learnt of structure, the art which not art but nature has hitherto concealed with its merciful covering."

Mr. Symons, of course, had an actress in mind, but his argument can be applied to singers as well, although it is safest to remember that much of the true beauty of the human voice inevitably departs with the youth of its owner. Still style in singing is not noticeably affected by age and an artist who possesses or who has acquired this quality very often can afford to make lewd gestures at Father Time. If good singing depended upon a full and sensuous tone, such artists as Ronconi, Victor Maurel, Max Heinrich, Ludwig Wullner, and Maurice Renaud would never have had any careers at all. It is obvious that any true estimate of their contribution to the lyric stage would put the chief emphasis on style, and this is usually the explanation for extended success on the opera or concert stage, although occasionally an extraordinary and exceptional singer may continue to give pleasure to her auditors, despite the fact that she has left middle age behind her, by the mere lovely quality of the tone she produces.

In the history of opera there may be found the names of many singers who have maintained their popularity and, indeed, a good deal of their art, long past fifty, and there is recorded at least one instance in which a singer, after a long absence from the theatre, returned to the scene of her earlier triumphs with her powers unimpaired, even augmented. I refer, of course, to Henrietta Sontag, born in 1805, who retired from the stage of the King's Theatre in London in 1830 in her twenty-fifth year and who returned twenty years later in 1849. She had, in the meantime, become the Countess Rossi, but although she had abandoned the stage her reappearance proved that she had not remained idle during her period of retirement. For she was one of those artists in whom early "inspiration" counted for little and "method" for much. She was, indeed, a mistress of style. She came back to the public in **Linda di Chaminoux** and H. F. Chorley ("Thirty Years' Musical Recollections") tells us that "all went wondrously well. No magic could restore to her voice an upper note or two which Time had taken; but the skill, grace, and precision with which she turned to account every atom of power she still possessed,--the incomparable steadiness with which she wrought out her composer's intentions--she carried through the part, from first to last, without the slightest failure, or sign of weariness--seemed a triumph. She was greeted--as she deserved to be--as a beloved old friend come home again in the late sunnier days.

"But it was not at the moment of Madame Sontag's reappearance that we could advert to all the difficulty which added to the honour of its success.--She came back under musical conditions entirely changed since she left the stage--to an orchestra far stronger than that which had supported her voice when it was younger; and to a new world of operas.--Into this she ventured with an intrepid industry not to be overpraised--with every new part enhancing the respect of every real lover of music.--During the short period of these new performances at Her Majesty's Theatre, which was not equivalent to two complete Opera seasons, not merely did Madame Sontag go through the range of her old characters--Susanna, Rosina, Desdemona, Donna Anna, and the like--but she presented herself in seven or eight operas which had not existed when she left the stage--Bellini's **Sonnambula**, Donizetti's **Linda**, **La Figlia del Reggimento**, **Don Pasquale**; **Le Tre Nozze**, of Signor Alary, **La Tempesta**, by M. Halevy--the last two works involving what the French call 'creation,' otherwise the production of a part never before represented.--In one of the favourite characters of her predecessor, the elder artist beat the younger one hollow.--This was as Maria, in Donizetti's **La Figlia**, which Mdlle. Lind may be said to have brought to England, and considered as her special property.... With myself, the real value of Madame Sontag grew, night after night--as her variety, her conscientious steadiness, and her adroit use of diminished powers were thus mercilessly tested. In one respect, compared with every one who had been in my time, she was alone, in right, perhaps of the studies of her early days--as a singer of Mozart's music."

It was after these last London seasons that Mme. Sontag undertook an American tour. She died in Mexico.

The great Mme. Pasta's ill-advised return to the stage in 1850 (when

she made two belated appearances in London) is matter for sadder
comment. Chorley, indeed, is at his best when he writes of it, his pen
dipped in tears, for none had admired this artist in her prime more
passionately than he. Here was a particularly good opportunity to
study the bare skeleton of interpretative art; the result is one of
the most striking passages in all literature:

"Her voice, which at its best, had required ceaseless watching and
practice, had been long ago given up by her. Its state of utter ruin
on the night in question passes description.--She had been neglected
by those who, at least, should have presented her person to the best
advantage admitted by Time.--Her queenly robes (she was to sing some
scenes from *Anna Bolena*) in nowise suited or disguised her figure.
Her hair-dresser had done some tremendous thing or other with her
head--or rather had left everything undone. A more painful and
disastrous spectacle could hardly be looked on.--There were artists
present, who had then, for the first time, to derive some impression
of a renowned artist--perhaps, with the natural feeling that her
reputation had been exaggerated.--Among these was Rachel--whose bitter
ridicule of the entire sad show made itself heard throughout the whole
theatre, and drew attention to the place where she sat--one might even
say, sarcastically enjoying the scene. Among the audience, however,
was another gifted woman, who might far more legitimately have been
shocked at the utter wreck of every musical means of expression in the
singer--who might have been more naturally forgiven, if some humour of
self-glorification had made her severely just--not worse--to an old
prima donna;--I mean Madame Viardot.--Then, and not till then, she
was hearing Madame Pasta.--But Truth will always answer to the appeal
of Truth. Dismal as was the spectacle--broken, hoarse, and destroyed
as was the voice--the great style of the singer spoke to the great
singer. The first scene was Ann Boleyn's duet with Jane Seymour. The
old spirit was heard and seen in Madame Pasta's *Sorgi!* and the
gesture with which she signed to her penitent rival to rise. Later,

she attempted the final mad scene of the opera--that most complicated and brilliant among the mad scenes on the modern musical stage--with its two *cantabile* movements, its snatches of recitative, and its *bravura* of despair, which may be appealed to as an example of vocal display, till then unparagoned, when turned to the account of frenzy, not frivolity--perhaps as such commissioned by the superb creative artist.--By that time, tired, unprepared, in ruin as she was, she had rallied a little. When--on Ann Boleyn's hearing the coronation music of her rival, the heroine searches for her own crown on her brow--Madame Pasta turned in the direction of the festive sounds, the old irresistible charm broke out;--nay, even in the final song, with its *roulades*, and its scales of shakes, ascending by a semi-tone, the consummate vocalist and tragedian, able to combine form with meaning--the moment of the situation, with such personal and musical display as form an integral part of operatic art--was indicated: at least to the apprehension of a younger artist.--'You are right!' was Madame Viardot's quick and heartfelt response (her eyes were full of tears) to a friend beside her--'You are right! It is like the *Cenacolo* of Da Vinci at Milan--a wreck of a picture, but the picture is the greatest picture in the world!'"

The great Mme. Viardot herself, whose intractable voice and noble stage presence inevitably remind one of Mme. Pasta, took no chances with fate. The friend of Alfred de Musset, the model for George Sand's "Consuelo," the "creator" of Fides in *Le Prophete*, and the singer who, in the revival of *Orphee* at the Theatre Lyrique in 1859, resuscitated Gluck's popularity in Paris, retired from the opera stage in 1863 at the age of 43, shortly after she had appeared in *Alceste!* (She sang in concert occasionally until 1870 or later.) Thereafter she divided her time principally between Baden and Paris and became the great friend of Turgeniev. His very delightful letters to her have been published. Idleness was abhorrent to this fine woman and in her middle and old age she gave lessons, while singers, composers, and conductors alike came to her for help and advice. She died in 1910 at the age of 89. Her less celebrated brother, Manuel Garcia (less celebrated as a singer; as a teacher he is given the credit for having restored Jenny Lind's voice. Among his other pupils Mathilde Marchesi and Marie Tempest may be mentioned), had died in 1906 at the age of 101. Her sister, Mme. Malibran, died very young, in the early Nineteenth Century, before, in fact, Mme. Viardot had made her debut.

Few singers have had the wisdom to follow Mme. Viardot's excellent example. The great Jenny Lind, long after her voice had lost its quality, continued to sing in oratorio and concert. So did Adelina Patti. Muriel Starr once told me of a parrot she encountered in Australia. The poor bird had arrived at the noble age of 117 and was entirely bereft of feathers. Flapping his stumpy wings he cried incessantly, "I'll fly, by God, I'll fly!" So, many singers, having lost their voices, continue to croak, "I'll sing, by God, I'll sing!" The Earl of Mount Edgcumbe, himself a man of considerable years when he published his highly diverting "Musical Reminiscences," gives us some extraordinary pictures of senility on the stage at the close of the Eighteenth Century. There was, for example, the case of Cecilia Davis, the first Englishwoman to sustain the part of prima donna and in that situation was second only to Gabrielli, whom she even rivalled in neatness of execution. Mount Edgcumbe found Miss Davies in Florence, unengaged and poor. A concert was arranged at which she appeared with her sister. Later she returned to England ... too old to secure an engagement. "This unfortunate woman is now (in 1834) living in London, in the extreme of old age, disease, and poverty," writes the Earl. He also speaks of a Signora Galli, of large and masculine figure and contralto voice, who frequently filled the part of second man at the Opera. She had been a principal singer in Handel's oratorios when conducted by himself. She afterwards fell into extreme poverty, and at the age of about seventy (!!!!), was induced to come forward to sing again at the oratorios. "I had the curiosity to go, and heard her sing *He was despised and rejected of men* in The Messiah. Of course her voice was cracked and trembling, but it was easy to see her school was good; and it was a pleasure to observe the kindness with which she was received and listened to; and to mark the animation and delight with which she seemed to hear again the music in which she had formerly been a distinguished performer. The poor old woman had been in the habit of coming to me annually for a trifling present; and she told me on that occasion that nothing but the severest distress should have compelled her so to expose herself, which after all, did not answer to its end, as she was not paid according to her agreement. She died shortly after." In 1783 the Earl heard a singer named Allegranti in Dresden, then at the height of her powers. Later she returned to England and reappeared in Cimarosa's *Matrimonio Segreto*. "Never was there a more pitiable attempt: she had scarcely a thread of voice remaining, nor the power to sing a note in tune: her figure and acting were equally altered for the worse, and after a few nights she was obliged to retire and quit the stage altogether." The celebrated Madame Mara, after a long sojourn in Russia, suddenly returned to England and was announced for a benefit performance at the King's Theatre after everybody had forgotten her existence. "She must have been at least seventy; but it was said that her voice had miraculously returned, and was as good as ever. But when she displayed those wonderfully revived powers, they proved, as might have been expected, lamentably deficient, and the tones she produced were compared to those of a *penny trumpet*. Curiosity was so little excited that the concert was ill attended ... and Madame Mara was heard no more. I was not so lucky (or so unlucky) as to hear these her last notes, as it was early in the winter, and I was not in town. She returned to Russia, and was a great sufferer by the burning of Moscow. After that she lived at Mitlau, or some other town near the Baltic, where she died at a great age, not many years ago."

Here is Michael Kelly's account of the same event: "With all her great skill and knowledge of the world, Madame Mara was induced, by the advice of some of her mistaken friends, to give a public concert at the King's Theatre, in her seventy-second year, when, in the course of nature her powers had failed her. It was truly grievous to see such transcendent talents as she once possessed, so sunk--so fallen. I used every effort in my power to prevent her committing herself, but in vain. Among other arguments to draw her from her purpose, I told her what happened to Monbelli, one of the first tenors of his day, who lost all his well-earned reputation and fame, by rashly performing the part of a lover, at the Pergola Theatre, at Florence, in his seventieth year, having totally lost his voice. On the stage, he was hissed; and the following lines, lampooning his attempt, were chalked on his house-door, as well as upon the walls of the city:--

> 'All' eta di settanta
> Non si ama, ne si canta.'"

W. T. Parke, forty years principal oboe player at Covent Garden Theatre, is kinder to Madame Mara in his "Musical Memoirs," but it must be taken into account that he is kinder to every one else, too. There is little of the acrimonious or the fault-finding note in his pages. This is his version of the affair: "That extraordinary singer of former days, Madame Mara, who had passed the last eighteen years in Russia, and who had lately arrived in England, gave a concert at the King's Theatre on the 6th of March (1820), which highly excited the curiosity of the musical public. On that occasion she sang some of her best airs; and though her powers were greatly inferior to what they were in her zenith, yet the same pure taste pervaded her performance. Whether vanity or interest stimulated Mara at her time of life to that undertaking, it would be difficult to determine; but whichsoever had the ascendency, her reign was short; for by singing one night afterwards at the vocal concert, the veil which had obscured her judgment was removed, and she retired to enjoy in private life those comforts which her rare talent had procured for her."

Parke also speaks of a Mrs. Pinto, "the once celebrated Miss Brent, the original Mandane in Arne's ***Artaxerxes***," who appeared in 1785 at the age of nearly seventy in Milton's ***Mask of Comus*** at a benefit for a Mr. Hull, "the respectable stage-manager of Covent Garden Theatre." She was to sing the song of Sweet Echo and as Parke was to play the responses to her voice on the oboe he repaired to her house for rehearsal. "Although nearly seventy years old, her voice possessed the remains of those qualities for which it had been so much celebrated,--power, flexibility, and sweetness. On the night ***Comus*** was performed she sung with an unexpected degree of excellence, and was loudly applauded. This old lady, as a singer, gave me the idea of a fine piece of ruins, which though considerably dilapidated, still displayed some of its original beauties."

The celebrated Faustina, whose quarrel with Cuzzoni is as famous in the history of music as the war between Gluck and Piccinni, was less daring. Dr. Burney visited her when she was seventy-two years old and asked her to sing. "Alas, I cannot," she replied, "I have lost all my faculties."

La Camargo, the favourite dancer of Paris in the early Eighteenth Century, the inventor, indeed of the short ballet skirt, and the possessor of many lovers, retired from the stage in 1751 with a large fortune, besides a pension of fifteen hundred francs. Thenceforth she led a secluded life. She was an assiduous visitor to the poor of her parish and she kept a dozen dogs and an angora cat which she overwhelmed with affection. In that quaint book, "The Powder Puff," by Franz Blei, you may find a most charming description of a call paid to the lady in 1768 in her little old house in the Rue St. Thomas du Louvre, by Duclos, Grimm, and Helvetius, who had come in bantering mood to ask her whom, in her past life, she had loved best. Her reply touched these men, who took their leave. "Helvetius told Camargo's story to his wife; Grimm made a note of it for his Court Journal; and as for Duclos, it suggested some moral reflections to him, for when, two years later, Mlle. Marianne Camargo was carried to her grave, he remarked: 'It is quite fitting to give her a white pall like a virgin.'"

Sophie Arnould, one of the most celebrated actresses and singers of the Eighteenth Century, died in poverty at the age of 63 and there is no record of her burial place. She had been the friend of Voltaire, Rousseau, d'Alembert, Diderot, Helvetius, and the Baron d'Holbach. She had "created" Gluck's *Iphigenie en Aulide* and the composer had said of her, "If it had not been for the voice and elocution of Mlle. Arnould, my *Iphigenie* would never have been performed in France." In her youth she had interested not only Marie Antoinette but also the King, and she had been the object of Mme. de Pompadour's suspicion and Mme. du Barry's rage. Garrick declared her a better actress than Clairon. She was as famous for her wit as for her singing and acting. When Mme. Laguerre appeared drunk in *Iphigenie en Tauride* she exclaimed, "Why this is *Iphigenie en Champagne!*" Indeed, she made so many remarks worthy of preservation that shortly after her death in 1802, a book called "Arnoldiana," devoted to her epigrams, was issued.... Nevertheless, this lady was hissed at the age of 36, when, after a short absence from the stage she reappeared as Iphigenie in 1776. She was neither old nor ugly and if her voice may have lost something her nineteen years of stage life in Paris might have weighed against that. On one occasion, according to La Harpe, when she had the line to sing, "You long for me to be gone," the audience applauded vociferously. To protect Sophie, Marie Antoinette sat in a box on several nights and stemmed the storm of disapproval, but in the end even the presence of the queen herself was insufficient to quell the hissing. One sad story completes the picture. In 1785, when her financial troubles were beginning, her two sons, who bore her no love, called for money. She had none to give them. "There are two horses left in the stable," she said. "Take those." They rode away on the horses.

Latin audiences are notoriously unfaithful to their stage favourites. In "The Innocents Abroad" Mark Twain tells us of the bad manners of an Italian audience. The singer he mentions is Erminia Frezzolini, born at Orvieto in 1818. She sang both in England and America. Chorley said of her: "She was an elegant, tall woman, born with a lovely voice, and bred with great vocal skill (of a certain order); but she was the first who arrived of the 'young Italians'--of those who fancy that driving the voice to its extremities can stand in the stead of passion. But she was, nevertheless, a real singer, and her art stood her in stead for some years after nature broke down. When she had left her scarce a note of her rich and real soprano voice to scream with, Madame Frezzolini was still charming." She died in Paris, November 5, 1884. Now for Mark Twain:

"I said I knew nothing against the upper classes from personal observation. I must recall it. I had forgotten. What I saw their bravest and their fairest do last night, the lowest multitude that could be scraped out of the purlieus of Christendom would blush to do, I think. They assembled by hundreds, and even thousands, in the great Theatre of San Carlo to do--what? Why simply to make fun of an old woman--to deride, to hiss, to jeer at an actress they once worshipped, but whose beauty is faded now, and whose voice has lost its former richness. Everybody spoke of the rare sport there was to be. They said the theatre would be crammed because Frezzolini was going to sing. It was said she could not sing well now, but then the people liked to see her, anyhow. And so we went. And every time the woman sang they hissed and laughed--the whole magnificent house--and as soon as she left the stage they called her on again with applause. Once or twice she was encored five and six times in succession, and received with hisses

when she appeared, and discharged with hisses and laughter when she
had finished--then instantly encored and insulted again! And how the
high-born knaves enjoyed it! White-kidded gentlemen and ladies laughed
till the tears came, and clapped their hands in very ecstasy when that
unhappy old woman would come meekly out for the sixth time, with
uncomplaining patience, to meet a storm of hisses! It was the
cruellest exhibition--the most wanton, the most unfeeling. The singer
would have conquered an audience of American rowdies by her brave,
unflinching tranquillity (for she answered encore after encore, and
smiled and bowed pleasantly, and sang the best she possibly could, and
went bowing off, through all the jeers and hisses, without ever losing
countenance or temper); and surely in any other land than Italy her
sex and her helplessness must have been an ample protection for
her--she could have needed no other. Think what a multitude of small
souls were crowded into that theatre last night!"

English audiences, on the other hand, are notoriously friendly to
their old favourites. When Dr. Hanslick, the Viennese critic, visited
England and heard Sims Reeves singing before crowded houses as he had
been doing for forty or fifty years, he remarked, "It is not easy to
win the favour of the English public; to lose it is quite impossible."

Mme. Grisi made her last appearance in London in 1866 at the theatre
she had left twenty years previously, Her Majesty's. The opera was
Lucrezia Borgia. At the end of the first act she miscalculated the
depth of the apron and the descending curtain left her outside on her
knees. She had stiffness in her joints and was unable to rise without
assistance.... This situation must have been very embarassing to a
singer who previously had been an idol of the public. In the
passionate duet with the tenor she made an unsuccessful attempt to
reach the A natural. Notwithstanding the fact that she was well
received and that she got through with the greater part of the opera
with credit, her impressario, J. H. Mapleson, relates in his "Memoirs"

that after the final curtain had fallen she rushed to tell him that it was all over and that she would never appear again. In "Student and Singer" Charles Santley writes of the occasion: "I had been singing at the Crystal Palace concert in the afternoon, and after dining there I went up to the theatre to see a little of the performance. I felt very sorry for Grisi that she had been induced to appear again; it was a sad sight for any one who had known her in her prime, and even long past it."

However, even English audiences can be cold. John E. Cox, in his "Musical Recollections," recalls an earlier occasion when Grisi sang at the Crystal Palace without much success (July 31, 1861): "On retiring from the orchestra, after a peculiarly cold reception--as unkind as it was inconsiderate, seeing what the career of this remarkable woman had been--there was not a single person at the foot of the orchestra to receive or to accompany her to her retiring room! I could imagine what her feelings at that moment must have been--she who had in former years been accustomed to be thronged, wherever she appeared, and to be the recipient of adulation--often as exaggerated as it was fulsome--but who was now literally deserted. With Grisi--although I had been once or twice introduced to her--I never had any personal acquaintance. I could not, however, resist the impulse of preceding her, without obtruding myself on her notice, and opening the door of the retiring room for her, which was situated at some considerable distance from the orchestra. Her look as I did this, and she passed out of sight, is amongst the most painful of my 'Recollections.'"

German audiences are usually kind to their favourites. In America we adopt neither the attitude of the English and Germans, nor yet that of the Italians and French. We simply stay away from the theatre. Mark Twain has put it succinctly, "When a singer has lost his voice and a jumper his legs, those parties fail to draw."

Benjamin Lumley in his "Reminiscences of the Opera," quoting an anonymous friend, relates a touching story regarding Catalani, who was born in 1779 and who retired from the stage in 1831. When Jenny Lind visited Paris in the spring of 1849 she learned to her astonishment that Catalani was in the French capital. The old singer, who resided habitually in Florence, had come to Paris with her daughter who, as the widow of a Frenchman, was obliged to go through certain legal forms before taking possession of her share of her husband's property. Through a friend of both ladies it was arranged that the two should meet at a dinner at the home of the Marquis of Normansby, the English ambassador to the Tuscan court, but the Swedish singer could not restrain her impatience and before that event she set out one forenoon for Mme. Catalani's apartment in the Rue de la Paix and sent in her name by a servant. The old singer hastened out to greet her distinguished visitor with obvious delight. She had known nothing of Mlle. Lind's presence in Paris and had feared that such a chance would never befall her, much as she had longed to see the celebrated singer who had excited the English public in a way which recalled her own past triumphs and who rivalled her in her purity and her charity. They talked together for an hour.... At the dinner the Marchioness of Normansby considerately refrained from asking Jenny Lind to sing, because no one is allowed to refuse such an invitation made by a representative of royalty. Catalani, however, had no such scruples. She went up to the Nightingale and begged her to sing, adding, "C'est la vieille Catalini qui desire vous entendre chanter, avant de mourir!" This appeal was irresistible. Jenny Lind sat down to the piano and sang *Non credea mirarti* and one or two other airs, including *Ah! non giunge*. Catalani is described as sitting on an ottoman in the centre of the room, rocking her body to and fro with delight and sympathy, murmuring, "Ah la bella cosa che la musica, quando si fa di quella maniera!*" and again* "Ah! la carissima! quanto bellissima!" A dinner at Catalani's apartment followed, but a few days later it became known that the old singer was ill, an illness which proved fatal. She had, however, heard the Swedish Nightingale sing "*avant de mourir*."

William Gardiner visited Madame Catalani in 1846. "I was surprised at the vigour of Madame Catalani," he says, "and how little she has altered since I saw her in Derby in 1828. I paid her a compliment on her good looks. 'Ah,' said she, 'I'm sixty-six!' She has lost none of that commanding expression which gave her such dignity on the stage. She is without a wrinkle, and appears to be no more than forty. Her breadth of chest is still remarkable: it is this which endowed her with the finest voice that ever sang. Her speaking voice and dramatic air are still charming, and not in the least impaired."

Is Christine Nilsson still alive? I think so. She was born August 20, 1843. In Clara Louise Kellogg's very entertaining, but not always trustworthy, "Memoirs" there is an interesting reference to this singer in her later career. Dates, unfortunately, are not furnished. "I was present," declares Mme. Kellogg, "on the night ... when she practically murdered the high register of her voice. She had five upper notes the quality of which was unlike any other I ever heard and that possessed a peculiar charm. The tragedy happened during a performance of *The Magic Flute* in London.... Nilsson was the Queen of the Night, one of her most successful early roles. The second aria in *The Magic Flute* is more famous and less difficult than the first aria, and also, more effective. Nilsson knew well the ineffectiveness of the ending of the first aria in the two weakest notes of a soprano's voice, A natural and B flat. I never could understand why a master like Mozart should have chosen to use them as he did. There is no climax to the song. One has to climb up hard and fast and then stop short in the middle. It is an appalling thing to do and that night Nilsson took those two notes at the last in *chest tones*. 'Great heavens!' I gasped, 'what is she doing? What is the woman thinking of!' Of course I knew she was doing it to get volume and vibration and to give that trying climax some character. But to say that it was a fatal attempt is to put it mildly. She absolutely killed a certain quality in her voice there and then and she *never recovered it*. Even that night she had to cut out the second great aria. Her beautiful high notes were gone forever." As I have said, the date of this incident, which, so far as I know, is not recorded elsewhere, is not mentioned, but Christine Nilsson sang in New York in the early Eighties and continued to sing until 1891, the year of her final appearance in London.

Adelina Patti, born the same year as Nilsson but six months before (February 10, 1843; according to some records, which by no means go undisputed, a quartet of famous singers came into the world this year. The other two were Ilma de Murska and Pauline Lucca) made many farewell tours of this country ... one too many in 1903-4, when she displayed the *beaux restes* of her voice. She is living at present in retirement at Craig-y-Nos in Wales. Her greatest rival, Etelka Gerster, too, is alive, I believe.

Lilli Lehmann, one of the oldest of the living great singers, was born May 13, 1848. She was a member of the famous casts which introduced many of the Wagner works to New York. Her last appearances in opera here were made, I think, in the late Nineties, but she has sung here since in concert and in Germany she has frequently assisted at the performances of the Mozart festivals at Salzburg and has even sung in *Norma* and *Gotterdammerung* within recent years! Her head is now crowned with white hair and her noble appearance and magnificent style in singing have doubtless stood her in good stead at these belated performances, which probably were disappointing, judged as vocal exhibitions.

Lillian Nordica had a long career. She was born May 12, 1859, and made

her operatic debut in Brescia in *La Traviata* in 1879. She continued
to sing up to the time of her death in Batavia, Java, May 10, 1914.
Indeed she was then undertaking a concert tour of the world at the age
of 55! But the artist, who in the Nineties had held the Metropolitan
Opera House stage with honour in the great dramatic roles, had very
little to offer in her last years. Never a great musician, defects in
style began to make themselves evident as her vocal powers decreased.
Her season at the Manhattan Opera House in 1907-8 was quickly and
unpleasantly terminated. A subsequent single appearance as Isolde at
the Metropolitan in the winter of 1909-10 was even less successful.
The voice had lost its resonance, the singer her appeal. Her
magnificent courage and indomitable ambition urged her on to the end.

Two singers whose voices have been miraculously preserved, who have
indeed suffered little from the ravages of time, are Marcella Sembrich
and Nellie Melba. Both of these singers, however, have consistently
refrained from misusing their voices (if one may except the one
occasion on which Mme. Melba attempted to sing Brunnhilde in
Siegfried with disastrous results). Mme. Melba (according to Grove's
Dictionary, which, like all other books devoted to the subject of
music, is frequently inaccurate) was born in Australia, May 19, 1859.
Therefore she was 28 years old when she made her debut in Brussels as
Gilda on October 12, 1887. She has used her voice carefully and well
and still sings in concert and opera at the age of 59. With the
advance of age, indeed, her voice began to take on colour. When she
sang here in opera at the Manhattan Opera House in 1906-7 she was in
her best vocal estate. Her voice, originally rather pale, had become
mellow and rich, although it is possible it had lost some of its old
remarkable agility. When last I listened to her in concert, a few
years ago at the Hippodrome, it seemed to me that I had never before
heard so beautiful a voice, and yet Mme. Melba sang in the first
performance of opera I ever attended (Chicago Auditorium; *Faust*,
February 22, 1899).

According to H. T. Finck, Caruso once said, "When you hear that an artist is going to retire, don't you believe it, for as long as he keeps his voice he will sing. You may depend upon that." Sometimes, indeed, longer. Mme. Melba made a belated and unfortunate attempt to sing Marguerite in *Faust* with the Chicago Opera Company, Monday evening, February 4, 1918, at the Lexington Theatre, New York. She sang with some art and style; her tone was still pure and her wonderful enunciation still remained a feature of her performance but scarcely a shadow of the beautiful voice I can remember so well was left. As if to atone for vocal deficiencies the singer made histrionic efforts such as she had never deemed necessary during the height of her career. Her meeting with Faust in the Kermesse scene was accomplished with modesty that almost became fright. She nearly danced the jewel song and embraced the tenor with passion in the love duet. In the church scene, overcome with terror at the sight of Mephistopheles, she flung her prayer book across the stage.... Her appearance was almost shocking and the first lines of the part of Marguerite, "*Non monsieur, je ne suis demoiselle, ni belle*" had a merciless application. However, the audience received her with kindness, more with a certain sort of enthusiasm. She reappeared again in the same opera on Thursday evening, February 14, 1918, but on this occasion I did not hear her.

Marcella Sembrich was born February 15, 1858. She made her debut in Athens in *I Puritani*, June 8, 1877, and she made her New York debut in *Lucia* October 24, 1883, at the beginning of the first season of the Metropolitan Opera House. After a long absence she returned to New York in 1898 as Rosina in *Il Barbiere*. After that year she sang pretty steadily at the Metropolitan until February 6, 1909, when, at the age of 51 (or lacking nine days of it), she bid farewell to the New York opera stage in acts from several of her favourite operas. She subsequently sang in a few performances of opera in Europe and was heard in song recital in America. When she left the opera house she had no rival in vocal artistry; and she had so satisfactorily solved the problems of style in singing certain kinds of songs that she also surveyed the field of song recital from a mountain top.... But such a singer as Mme. Sembrich, who made her appeal through the expression of the milder emotions, who never, indeed, attempted to touch dramatic depths, even style, in the end, will not assist. Magnificent Lilli Lehmann might make a certain effect in *Gotterdammerung* so long as she had a leg to stand on or a note to croak, but an adequate delivery of *Der Nussbaum* or *Wie Melodien* demands a vocal control which a singer past middle age is not always sure of possessing.... After a long retirement, Mme. Sembrich gave a concert at Carnegie Hall, November 21, 1915. The house was crowded and the applause at the beginning must almost have unnerved the singer, who walked slowly towards the front of the platform as the storm burst and then bowed her head again and again. Her program on this occasion was not one of her best. She had not chosen familiar songs in which to return to her public. This may in a measure account for her lack of success in always calling forth steady tones. However, on the whole, her voice sounded amazingly fresh. Her high notes especially rang true and resonant as ever. Her middle voice showed wear. Her style remained impeccable, unrivalled.... She announced, following this concert, a series of four recitals in a small hall and actually appeared at one of them. This time I did not hear her, but I am told that her voice refused to respond to her wishes. Nor was the hall filled. The remaining concerts were abandoned. "Mme. Sembrich has never been a failure and she is too old to begin now!" she is reported to have said to a friend.

Emma Calve's date of birth is recorded as 1864 in some of the musical dictionaries. This would make her 53 years old. Her singing of the *Marseillaise* a year ago at the Allies Bazaar at the Grand Central Palace proved to me that her retirement from the Opera was premature.

Her performances at the Manhattan Opera House in 1906-7 were memorable, vocally superb. Her Carmen was out of drawing dramatically, but her Anita and her Santuzza remained triumphs of stage craft.

Emma Eames, born August 13, 1867, is three years younger than Mme. Calve. She made her debut as Juliette, March 13, 1889. She retired from the opera stage in 1907-8, although she has sung since then a few times in concert. Her last appearances at the Opera were made in dramatic roles, Donna Anna, Leonora (in *Trovatore*), and Tosca, in contradistinction to the lyric parts in which she gained her early fame. That she was entirely successful in compassing the breach cannot be said in all justice. Yet there was a certain distinction in her manner, a certain acid quality in her voice, that gave force to these characterizations. Certainly, however, no one would ever have compared her Donna Anna favourably with her Countess in *Figaro*. Her performance of *Or sai chi l'onore* was deficient in breadth of style and her lack of breath control at this period gave uncertainty to her execution.

Life teaches us, through experience, that no rule is infallible, but insofar as I am able to give a meaning to these rambling biographical notes, collected, I may as well admit, more to interest my reader than to prove anything, it is the meaning, sounded with a high note of truth, by Arthur Symons, in the paragraph quoted at the beginning of this essay. Style is a rare quality in a singer. With it in his possession an artist may dare much for a long time. Without it he exists as long as those qualities which are perfectly natural to him exist. A voice fades, but a manner of applying that voice (even when there is practically no voice to apply) to an artistic problem has an indefinite term of life.

Yvette Guilbert once told me that crossing the Atlantic with Duse on one occasion she had asked the Italian actress if she were going to include **La Dame aux Camelias** in her American repertory. "I am too old to play Marguerite ..." was the sad response. "She was right," said Guilbert, in relating the incident, "she was too old; she was born too old ... in spirit. Now when I am sixty-three I shall begin to impersonate children. I grow younger every year!"

September 12, 1917.

Impressions in the Theatre

I

The Land of Joy

> "Dancing is something more than an amusement in Spain. It is part of that solemn ritual which enters into the whole life of the people. It expresses their very spirit."

Havelock Ellis.

An idle observer of theatrical conditions might derive a certain ironic pleasure from remarking the contradiction implied in the professed admiration of the constables of the playhouse for the unconventional and their almost passionate adoration for the conventional. We constantly hear it said that the public cries for novelty, and just as constantly we see the same kind of acting, the same gestures, the same Julian Mitchellisms and George Marionisms and Ned Wayburnisms repeated in and out of season, summer and winter. Indeed, certain conventions (which bore us even now) are so deeply rooted in the soil of our theatre that I see no hope of their being eradicated before the year 1999, at which date other conventions will have supplanted them and will likewise have become tiresome.

In this respect our theatre does not differ materially from the theatres of other countries except in one particular. In Europe the juxtaposition of nations makes an interchange of conventions possible, which brings about slow change or rapid revolution. Paris, for example, has received visits from the Russian Ballet which almost assumed the proportions of Tartar invasions. London, too, has been invaded by the Russians and by the Irish. The Irish playwrights, indeed, are continually pounding away at British middle-class complacency. Germany, in turn, has been invaded by England (we regret that this sentence has only an artistic and figurative significance), and we find Max Reinhardt well on his way toward giving a complete cycle of the plays of Shakespeare; a few years ago we might have observed Deutschland groveling hysterically before Oscar Wilde's *Salome*, a play which, at least without its musical dress, has not, I believe, even yet been performed publicly in London. In Italy, of course, there are no artistic invasions (nobody cares to pay for them) and even the conventions of the Italian theatre themselves, such as the *Commedia del' Arte*, are quite dead; so the country remains as dormant, artistically speaking, as a rag rug, until an enthusiast like Marinetti arises to take it between his teeth and shake it back into rags again.

Very often whisperings of art life in the foreign theatre (such as accounts of Stanislavski's accomplishments in Moscow) cross the Atlantic. Very often the husks of the realities (as was the case with the Russian Ballet) are imported. But whispers and husks have about as much influence as the "New York Times" in a mayoralty campaign, and as a result we find the American theatre as little aware of world activities in the drama as a deaf mute living on a pole in the desert of Sahara would be. Indeed any intrepid foreign investigator who wishes to study the American drama, American acting, and American stage decoration will find them in almost as virgin a condition as they were in the time of Lincoln.

A few rude assaults have been made on this smug eupepsy. I might mention the coming of Paul Orleneff, who left Alla Nazimova with us to be eventually swallowed up in the conventional American theatre. Four or five years ago a company of Negro players at the Lafayette Theatre gave a performance of a musical revue that boomed like the big bell in the Kremlin at Moscow. Nobody could be deaf to the sounds. Florenz Ziegfeld took over as many of the tunes and gestures as he could buy for his ***Follies*** of that season, but he neglected to import the one essential quality of the entertainment, its style, for the exploitation of which Negro players were indispensable. For the past two months Mimi Aguglia, one of the greatest actresses of the world, has been performing in a succession of classic and modern plays (a repertory comprising dramas by Shakespeare, d'Annunzio, and Giacosa) at the Garibaldi Theatre, on East Fourth Street, before very large and very enthusiastic audiences, but uptown culture and managerial acumen will not awaken to the importance of this gesture until they read about it in some book published in 1950....

All of which is merely by way of prelude to what I feel must be something in the nature of lyric outburst and verbal explosion. A few nights ago a Spanish company, unheralded, unsung, indeed almost unwelcomed by such reviewers as had to trudge to the out-of-the-way Park Theatre, came to New York, in a musical revue entitled The Land of Joy. ***The score was written by Joaquin Valverde,*** fils, whose music is not unknown to us, and the company included La Argentina, a

Spanish dancer who had given matinees here in a past season without
arousing more than mild enthusiasm. The theatrical impressarii, the
song publishers, and the Broadway rabble stayed away on the first
night. It was all very well, they might have reasoned, to read about
the goings on in Spain, but they would never do in America. Spanish
dancers had been imported in the past without awakening undue
excitement. Did not the great Carmencita herself visit America twenty
or more years ago? These impressarii had ignored the existence of a
great psychological (or more properly physiological) truth: you cannot
mix Burgundy and Beer! One Spanish dancer surrounded by Americans is
just as much lost as the great Nijinsky himself was in an English
music hall, where he made a complete and dismal failure. And so they
would have been very much astonished (had they been present) on the
opening night to have witnessed all the scenes of uncontrollable
enthusiasm--just as they are described by Havelock Ellis, Richard
Ford, and Chabrier--repeated. The audience, indeed, became hysterical,
and broke into wild cries of ***Ole! Ole!*** Hats were thrown on the
stage. The audience became as abandoned as the players, became a part
of the action.

You will find all this described in "The Soul of Spain," in
"Gatherings from Spain," in Chabrier's letters, and it had all been
transplanted to New York almost without a whisper of preparation,
which is fortunate, for if it had been expected, doubtless we would
have found the way to spoil it. Fancy the average New York first-night
audience, stiff and unbending, sceptical and sardonic, welcoming this
exhibition! Havelock Ellis gives an ingenious explanation for the fact
that Spanish dancing has seldom if ever successfully crossed the
border of the Iberian peninsula: "The finest Spanish dancing is at
once killed or degraded by the presence of an indifferent or
unsympathetic public, and that is probably why it cannot be
transplanted, but remains local." Fortunately the Spaniards in the
first-night audience gave the cue, unlocked the lips and loosened the

hands of us cold Americans. For my part, I was soon yelling *Ole!* louder than anybody else.

The dancer, Doloretes, is indeed extraordinary. The gipsy fascination, the abandoned, perverse bewitchery of this female devil of the dance is not to be described by mouth, typewriter, or quilled pen. Heine would have put her at the head of his dancing temptresses in his ballet of *Mephistophela* (found by Lumley too indecent for representation at Her Majesty's Theatre, for which it was written; in spite of which the scenario was published in the respectable "Revue de Deux Mondes"). In this ballet a series of dancing celebrities are exhibited by the female Mephistopheles for the entertainment of her victim. After Salome had twisted her flanks and exploited the prowess of her abdominal muscles to perfunctory applause, Doloretes would have heated the blood, not only of Faust, but of the ladies and gentlemen in the orchestra stalls, with the clicking of her heels, the clacking of her castanets, now held high over head, now held low behind her back, the flashing of her ivory teeth, the shrill screaming, electric magenta of her smile, the wile of her wriggle, the passion of her performance. And close beside her the sinuous Mazantinita would flaunt a garish tambourine and wave a shrieking fan. All inanimate objects, shawls, mantillas, combs, and cymbals, become inflamed with life, once they are pressed into the service of these senoritas, languorous and forbidding, indifferent and sensuous. Against these rude gipsies the refined grace and Goyaesque elegance of La Argentina stand forth in high relief, La Argentina, in whose hands the castanets become as potent an instrument for our pleasure as the violin does in the fingers of Jascha Heifetz. Bilbao, too, with his thundering heels and his tauromachian gestures, bewilders our highly magnetized senses. When, in the dance, he pursues, without catching, the elusive Doloretes, it would seem that the limit of dynamic effects in the theatre had been reached.

Here are singers! The limpid and lovely soprano of the comparatively placid Maria Marco, who introduces figurations into the brilliant music she sings at every turn. One indecent (there is no other word for it) chromatic oriental phrase is so strange that none of us can ever recall it or forget it! And the frantically nervous Luisita Puchol, whose eyelids spring open like the cover of a Jack-in-the-box, and whose hands flutter like saucy butterflies, sings suggestive popular ditties just a shade better than any one else I know of.

But *The Land of Joy* does not rely on one or two principals for its effect. The organization as a whole is as full of fire and purpose as the original Russian Ballet; the costumes themselves, in their blazing, heated colours, constitute the ingredients of an orgy; the music, now sentimental (the adaptability of Valverde, who has lived in Paris, is little short of amazing; there is a vocal waltz in the style of Arditi that Mme. Patti might have introduced into the lesson scene of *Il Barbiere*; there is another song in the style of George M. Cohan--these by way of contrast to the Iberian music), now pulsing with rhythmic life, is the best Spanish music we have yet heard in this country. The whole entertainment, music, colours, costumes, songs, dances, and all, is as nicely arranged in its crescendos and decrescendos, its prestos and adagios as a Mozart finale. The close of the first act, in which the ladies sweep the stage with long ruffled trains, suggestive of all the Manet pictures you have ever seen, would seem to be unapproachable, but the most striking costumes and the wildest dancing are reserved for the very last scene of all. There these bewildering senoritas come forth in the splendourous envelope of embroidered Manila shawls, and such shawls! Prehistoric African roses of unbelievable measure decorate a texture of turquoise, from which depends nearly a yard of silken fringe. In others mingle royal purple and buff, orange and white, black and the kaleidoscope! The revue, a sublimated form of zarzuela, is calculated, indeed, to hold you in a dangerous state of nervous excitement during the entire evening, to keep you awake for the rest of the night, and to entice you to the theatre the next night and the next. It is as intoxicating as vodka, as insidious as cocaine, and it is likely to become a habit, like these stimulants. I have found, indeed, that it appeals to all classes of taste, from that of a telephone operator, whose usual artistic debauch is the latest antipyretic novel of Robert W. Chambers, to that of the frequenter of the concert halls.

I cannot resist further cataloguing; details shake their fists at my memory; for instance, the intricate rhythms of Valverde's elaborately syncopated music (not at all like ragtime syncopation), the thrilling orchestration (I remember one dance which is accompanied by drum taps and oboe, nothing else!), the utter absence of tangos (which are Argentine), and habaneras (which are Cuban), most of the music being written in two-four and three-four time, and the interesting use of folk-tunes; the casual and very suggestive indifference of the dancers, while they are not dancing, seemingly models for a dozen Zuloaga paintings, the apparently inexhaustible skill and variety of these dancers in action, winding ornaments around the melodies with their feet and bodies and arms and heads and castanets as coloratura sopranos do with their voices. Sometimes castanets are not used; cymbals supplant them, or tambourines, or even fingers. Once, by some esoteric witchcraft, the dancers seemed to tap upon their arms. The effect was so stupendous and terrifying that I could not project myself into that aloof state of mind necessary for a calm dissection of its technique.

What we have been thinking of all these years in accepting the imitation and ignoring the actuality I don't know; it has all been down in black and white. What Richard Ford saw and wrote down in 1846 I am seeing and writing down in 1917. How these devilish Spaniards have been able to keep it up all this time I can't imagine. Here we have our paradox. Spain has changed so little that Ford's book is still the best to be procured on the subject (you may spend many a delightful half-hour with the charming irony of its pages for company). Spanish dancing is apparently what it was a hundred years ago; no wind from the north has disturbed it. Stranger still, it depends for its effect on the acquirement of a brilliant technique. Merely to play the castanets requires a severe tutelage. And yet it is all as spontaneous, as fresh, as unstudied, as vehement in its appeal, even to Spaniards, as it was in the beginning. Let us hope that Spain will have no artistic reawakening.

Aristotle and Havelock Ellis and Louis Sherwin have taught us that the theatre should be an outlet for suppressed desires. So, indeed, the ideal theatre should. As a matter of fact, in most playhouses (I will generously refrain from naming the one I visited yesterday) I am continually suppressing a desire to strangle somebody or other, but after a visit to the Spaniards I walk out into Columbus Circle completely purged of pity and fear, love, hate, and all the rest. It is an experience.

November 3, 1917.

II

A Note on Mimi Aguglia

> "Art has to do only with the creation of beauty, whether it
> be in words, or sounds, or colour, or outline, or rhythmical
> movement; and the man who writes music is no more truly an
> artist than the man who plays that music, the poet who
> composes rhythms in words no more truly an artist than the

dancer who composes rhythms with the body, and the one is no
more to be preferred to the other, than the painter is to be
preferred to the sculptor, or the musician to the poet, in
those forms of art which we have agreed to recognize as of
equal value."

Arthur Symons.

The only George Jean, "witty, wise, and cruel," and the "amaranthine"
Louis Sherwin, who understands better than anybody else how to plunge
the rapier into the vulnerable spot and twist it in the wound, making
the victim writhe, have been having some fun with the art of acting
lately, or to be exact, with the art of actors. Now actor-baiting is
no new game; as a winter sport it is as popular as making jokes about
mothers-in-law, decrying the art of Bouguereau or Howard Chandler
Christy, or discussing the methods of Mr. Belasco. Ever so long ago
(and George Henry Lewes preceded him) George Moore wrote an article
called "Mummer Worship," holding the players up to ridicule, but
George really adores the theatre and even acting, goes to the
playhouse constantly, and writes a bad play himself every few years.
None of these has achieved success on the stage. The list includes
Martin Luther, written with a collaborator, The Strike at
Arlingford, The Bending of the Bough (Moore's version of a play by
Edwin Martyn), a dramatization of "Esther Waters," *Elizabeth Cooper*,
and the fragment, *The Apostle*, on which "The Brook Kerith," was
based. Now he is at work turning the novel back into another play....
When the Sunday editor of a newspaper is at his wit's end he
invariably sends a competent reporter to collect data for a symposium
on one of two topics, Is the author or the player more important? or
Does the stage director make the actor? The amount of amusement this
reporter can derive in gathering indignant replies from mountebanks
and scribblers is only limited by his own sense of humour. Even the

late Sir Henry Irving felt compelled on more than one occasion to defend his "noble calling."

The actor, when he slaps back, usually overlooks the point at issue, but sometimes he has something to say over which we may well ponder. Witness, for example, the following passage, quoted from that justly celebrated compendium of personal opinions and broad-shaft wit called "Nat Goodwin's Book": "The average author and manager of today are prone to advertise themselves as conspicuously as the play (as if the public cared a snap who wrote the play or who 'presents'). I doubt if five per cent of the public know who wrote 'The Second Mrs. Tanqueray,' 'In Mizzoura,' or 'Richelieu,' but they know their stage favourites. I wonder how many mantels are adorned with pictures of the successful dramatist and those who 'present' and how many there are on which appear Maude Adams, Dave Warfield, Billie Burke, John Drew, Bernhardt, Duse, and hundreds of other distinguished players."

It is principally urged against the claims of acting as an art that a young person without previous experience or training can make an immediate (and sometimes lasting) effect upon the stage, whereas in the preparation for any other art (even the interpretative arts) years of training are necessary. This premise is full of holes; nevertheless George Moore, and Messrs. Nathan and Sherwin all cling to it. It is true that almost any young girl, moderately gifted with charm or comeliness, may make an instantaneous impression on our stage, especially in the namby-pamby roles which our playwrights usually give her to play. But she is soon found out. She may still attract audiences (as George Barr McCutcheon and Alma Tadema still attract audiences) but the discerning part of the public will take no joy in seeing her. Charles Frohman said (and he ought to know) that the average life of a female star on the American stage was ten years; in other words, her career continued as long as her youth and physical charms remained potent.

We have easily accounted for the unimportant actors, the rank and file, but what about those who immediately claim positions which they hold in spite of their lack of previous training? These are rarer. At the moment, indeed, I cannot think of any. For while genius often manifests itself early in a career, the great actors, as a rule, have struggled for many years to learn the rudiments of their art before they have given indisputable proof of their greatness, or before they have been recognized. "Real acting," according to Percy Fitzgerald, "is a science, to be studied and mastered, as other sciences are studied and mastered, by long years of training." They may not have had the strenuous Conservatoire and Theatre Francais training of Sarah Bernhardt. As a matter of fact, indeed, the actor may far better learn to handle his tools by manipulating them before an audience, than by practicing with them for too long a time in the closet. The technique of violin playing can best be acquired before the **virtuoso** appears in public, although no amount of training in itself will make a great violinist, but the basic elements of acting, grace, diction, etc., can just as well be acquired behind the footlights and so many great actors have acquired them, as many of the greatest have ignored them. There can be no hard and fast rules laid down for this sort of thing. Can we thank nine months with Mme. Marchesi for the instantaneous success and subsequent brilliant career of Mme. Melba? Against this training offset the years and years of road playing and the more years of study at home in retirement to account for the career of Mrs. Fiske. The Australian soprano was born with a naturally-placed and flexible voice. Her shake is said to have been perfection when she was a child; her scale was even; her intonation impeccable. She had very little to learn except the roles in the operas she was to sing and her future was very clearly marked from the night she made her debut as Gilda in **Rigoletto**. Mme. Patti was equally gifted. Mme. Pasta and Mme. Fremstad, on the other hand, toiled very slowly towards fame. The former singer was an absolute failure when she first appeared in

London and it took several years of hard work to make her the greatest lyric artist of her day. The great Jenny Lind retired from the stage completely defeated, only to return as the most popular singer of her time. Mischa Elman has told me he never practices; Leo Ornstein, on the other hand, spends hours every day at the piano. Mozart sprang, full-armed with genius, into the world. He began composing at the age of four. No training was necessary for him, but Beethoven and Wagner developed slowly. In the field of writers there are even more happy examples. Hundreds of boys have spent years in theme and literature courses in college preparing in vain for a future which was never to be theirs, while other youths with no educations have taken to writing as a cat takes to cat-nip. Should we assume that the annual output of Professor Baker's class at Harvard produces better playwrights than Moliere or Shakespeare, neither of whom enjoyed Professor Baker's lectures, nor, I think I am safe in conjecturing, anything like them?

What, after all, constitutes training? For a creative or interpretative genius mere existence seems to be sufficient. Joseph Conrad, Nicholas Rimsky-Korsakov, and Patrick MacGill all were sailors for many years before they began to write. We owe "Youth" and the first section of **Scheherazade** to this accident. MacGill also had the privilege of digging potatoes; he writes about it in "The Rat-pit." Mrs. Patrick Campbell learned enough about how to move about and how to speak in the country houses she frequented before she began her professional career to enable her immediately to take a position of importance on the stage. It does not seem necessary, indeed, that the training for any career should be prescribed or systematic. Some men get their training one way and some another. A school of acting may be of the greatest benefit to A, while B will not profit by it. Some actors are ruined by stock companies; others are improved by them. The geniuses in this interpretative art as in all the other interpretative and creative arts, seem to rise above obstructions, and to make themselves felt, whatever difficulties are put in their way.

Some great actors, like some great musicians and authors, create out of their fulness. They cannot explain; they do not need to study; they create by instinct. Others, like Beethoven and Olive Fremstad, work and rework their material in the closet until it approaches perfection, when they expose it. To say that there are bad actors following in the footsteps of both these types of geniuses is to be axiomatic and trite. It would be a foregone conclusion. Just as there are musicians who write as easily as Mozart but who have nothing to say, so there are other musicians who write and rewrite, work and rework, study and restudy, and yet what they finally offer the public has not the quality or the force or the inspiration of a common gutter-ballad.

It has also been urged in print that as naturalness is the goal of the actor he should never have to strive for it. The names of Frank Reicher and John Drew are often mentioned as those of men who "play themselves" on the stage. A most difficult thing to do! Also an unfortunate choice of names. Each of these artists has undergone a long and arduous apprenticeship in order to achieve the natural method which has given him eminence in his career. Indeed, of all the qualities of the actor this is the least easy to acquire.

Actors are often condemned because they are not versatile. Versatility is undoubtedly an admirable quality in an actor, valuable, especially to his manager, but hardly an essential one. An artist is not required to do more than one thing well. Vladimir de Pachmann specializes in Chopin playing, but Arthur Symons once wrote that "he is the greatest living pianist, because he can play certain things better than any other pianist can play anything." Should we not allot similar approval to the actor or actress who makes a fine effect in one part or in one kind of part? I should not call Ellen Terry a versatile actress, but I should call her a great artist. Marie Tempest

is not versatile, unless she should be so designated for having made
equal successes on the lyric and dramatic stages, but she is one of
the most satisfying artists at present appearing before our public.
Mallarme was not versatile; Cezanne was not versatile; nor was Thomas
Love Peacock. Mascagni, assuredly, is not versatile. The da Vincis and
Wagners are rare figures in the history of creative art just as the
Nijinskys and Rachels are rare in the history of interpretative art.

Someone may say that the great actor dies while the play goes
thundering on through the ages on the stage and in everyman's library.
This very point, indeed, is made by Mr. Lewes. But this, alas, is the
reverse of the truth. We have competent and immensely absorbing
records of the lives and art of David Garrick, Mrs. Siddons, Ristori,
Clairon, Rachel, Charlotte Cushman, Edwin Booth, and other prominent
players, while most of the plays in which they appeared are not only
no longer actable, but also no longer readable. The brothers de
Goncourt, for example, wrote an account of Clairon which is a book of
the first interest, while I defy any one to get through two pages of
most of the fustian she was compelled to act! The reason for this is
very easily formulated. Great acting is human and universal. It is
eternal in its appeal and its memory is easily kept alive while
playwrighting is largely a matter of fashion, and appeals to the mob
of men and women who never read and who are more interested in police
news than they are in poetry. George Broadhurst or Henry Bernstein or
Arthur Wing Pinero, or others like them, have always been the popular
playwrights; a few names like Sophocles, Terence, Moliere,
Shakespeare, and Ibsen come rolling down to us, but they are precious
and few.

A great actor, indeed, can put life into perfectly wooden material. In
the case of Sarah Bernhardt, who was the creator, the actress or
Sardou? In the case of Henry Irving, who was the creator, the actor or
the authors of *The Bells* and *Faust* (not, in this instance,

Goethe)? Is Langdon Mitchell's version of "Vanity Fair" sufficiently a work of art to exist without the co-operation of Mrs. Fiske? When Duse electrified her audiences in such plays as The Second Mrs. Tanqueray **and** Fedora, were the dramatists responsible for the effect? Arthur Symons says of her in the latter play, "A great actress, who is also a great intelligence, is seen accepting it, for its purpose, with contempt, as a thing to exercise her technical skill upon." One reads of Mrs. Siddone that she could move a roomful of people to tears merely by repeating the word "hippopotamus" with varying stress. Should we thank the behemoth for this miracle?

Any one who understands, great acting knows that it is illumination. There are those who are born to throw light on the creations of the poets, just as there are others born to be poets. These interpreters give a new life to the works of the masters, AEschylus, Congreve, Tchekhov. When, as more frequently happens, they are called upon to play mediocre parts it is with their own personal force, their atmospheric aura that they create something more than the author himself ever intended or dreamed of. How could Joseph Jefferson play *Rip Van Winkle* for thirty years (or longer) with scenery in tatters and a company of mummers which Corse Payton would have scorned? Was it because of the greatness of the play? If that were true, why is not some one else performing this drama today to large audiences? Has any one read the Joseph Jefferson acting version of *Rip Van Winkle*? Who wrote it? Don't you think it rather extraordinary that a play which apparently has given so much pleasure, and in which Jefferson was hailed as a great actor by every contemporary critic of note, as is in itself so little known? It is not extraordinary. It was Jefferson's performance of the title role which gave vitality to the play.

Of course, there are few actors who have this power, few great actors. What else could you expect? A critic might prove that playwriting was not an art on the majority of the evidence. Almost all the music composed in America could be piled up to prove that music was not an art. Should we say that there is no art of painting because the Germans have no great painters?

At present, however, it is quite possible for any one in New York with car or taxi-cab fare to see one of the greatest of living actresses. She is not playing on Broadway. This actress has never been to dramatic school; she has not had the advantages of Alla Nazimova, who has worked with at least one fine stage director. She was simply born a genius, that is all; she has perfected her art by appearing in a great variety of parts, the method of Edwin Booth. Most of these parts happen to be in masterpieces of the drama. She is not unaccustomed to playing *Zaza* one evening and d'Annunzio's *Francesca da Rimini* the next. Her repertory further includes *La Dame aux Camelias*, *Hamlet*, *Romeo and Juliet*, *La Figlia di Iorio*, Giuseppe Giacosa's Come le Foglie, Sicilian folk-plays, and plays by Arturo Giovannitti. When I first saw Mimi Aguglia she was little more than a crude force, a great struggling light, that sometimes illuminated, nay often blinded, but which shone in unequal flashes. Experience has made of her an actress who is almost unfailing in her effect. If you asked her about the technique of her art she would probably smile (as Mozart and Schubert might have done before her); if you asked her about her method she would not understand you ... but she understands the art of acting.

Watch her, for instance, in the second act of *Zaza*, in the scene in which the music hall singer discovers that her lover has a wife and child. No heroics, no shrieks, no conventional posturings and shruggings and sobbing ... something far worse she exposes to us, a nameless terror. She stands with her back against a table, nonchalant and smilingly defiant, unwilling to return to the music hall with her former partner, but pleasantly jocular in her refusal. Stung into anger, he hurls his last bomb. Zaza is smoking. As she listens to the cruel words the corner of her mouth twitches, the cigarette almost falls. That is all. There is a moment's silence unbroken save by the heartbeats of her spectators. Even the babies which mothers bring in abundance to the Italian theatre are quiet. With that esoteric magnetism with which great artists are possessed she holds the audience captive by this simple gesture. I could continue to point out other astounding details in this impersonation, but not one of them, perhaps, would illustrate Aguglia's art as does this one. If no training is necessary to produce effects of this kind, I would pronounce acting the most holy of the arts, for then, surely, it is a direct gift from God.

September 5, 1917.

III

The New Isadora

> "We shift and bedeck and bedrape us,
> Thou art noble and nude and antique;"

> Swinburne's "Dolores."

I have a fine memory of a chance description flung off by some one at a dinner in Paris; a picture of the youthful Isadora Duncan in her studio in New York developing her ideals through sheer will and preserving the contour of her feet by wearing carpet slippers. The latter detail stuck in my memory. It may or may not be true, but it could have been, ***should*** have been true. The incipient dancer keeping her feet pure for her coming marriage with her art is a subject for philosophic dissertation or for poetry. There are many poets who would have seized on this idea for an ode or even a sonnet, had it occurred to them. Oscar Wilde would have liked this excuse for a poem ... even Robert Browning, who would have woven many moral strophes from this text.... It would have furnished Mr. George Moore with material for another story for the volume called "Celibates." Walter Pater might have dived into some very beautiful, but very conscious, prose with this theme as a spring-board. Huysmans would have found this suggestion sufficient inspiration for a romance the length of "Clarissa Harlowe." You will remember that the author of "En Route" meditated writing a novel about a man who left his house to go to his office. Perceiving that his shoes have not been polished he stops at a boot-black's and during the operation he reviews his affairs. The problem was to make 300 pages of this!... Lombroso would have added the detail to his long catalogue in "The Man of Genius" as another proof of the insanity of artists. Georges Feydeau would have found therein enough matter for a three-act farce and d'Annunzio for a poetic drama which he might have dedicated to "Isadora of the beautiful feet." Sermons might be preached from the text and many painters would touch the subject with reverence. Manet might have painted Isadora with one of the carpet slippers half depending from a bare, rosy-white foot.

There are many fables concerning the beginning of Isadora's career. One has it that the original dance in bare feet was an accident.... Isadora was laving her feet in an upper chamber when her hostess begged her to dance for her other guests. Just as she was she descended and met with such approval that thenceforth her feet remained bare. This is a pretty tale, but it has not the fine ring of truth of the story of the carpet slippers. There had been bare-foot dancers before Isadora; there had been, I venture to say, discinct "Greek dancers." Isadora's contribution to her art is spiritual; it is her feeling for the idea of the dance which isolates her from her contemporaries. Many have overlooked this essential fact in attempting to account for her obvious importance. Her imitators (and has any other interpretative artist ever had so many?) have purloined her costumes, her gestures, her steps; they have put the music of Beethoven and Schubert to new uses as she had done before them; they have unbound their hair and freed their feet; but the essence of her art, the *spirit*, they have left in her keeping; they could not well do otherwise.

Inspired perhaps by Greek phrases, by the superb collection of Greek vases in the old Pinakotheck in Munich, Isadora cast the knowledge she had gleaned of the dancer's training from her. At least she forced it to be subservient to her new wishes. She flung aside her memory of the entrechat and the pirouette, the studied technique of the ballet; but in so doing she unveiled her own soul. She called her art the renaissance of the Greek ideal but there was something modern about it, pagan though it might be in quality. Always it was pure and sexless ... always abstract emotion has guided her interpretations.

In the beginning she danced to the piano music of Chopin and Schubert. Eleven years ago I saw her in Munich in a program of Schubert *impromptus* and Chopin *preludes* and *mazurkas*. A year or two later she was dancing in Paris to the accompaniment of the Colonne Orchestra, a good deal of the music of Gluck's *Orfeo* and the very lovely dances from *Iphigenie en Aulide*. In these she remained faithful to her original ideal, the beauty of abstract movement, the rhythm of exquisite gesture. This was not sense echoing sound but rather a very delightful confusion of her own mood with that of the music.

So a new grace, a new freedom were added to the dance; in her later representations she has added a third quality, strength. Too, her immediate interpretations often suggest concrete images.... A passionate patriotism for one of her adopted countries is at the root of her fiery miming of the *Marseillaise*, a patriotism apparently as deep-rooted, certainly as inflaming, as that which inspired Rachel in her recitation of this hymn during the Paris revolution of 1848. In times of civil or international conflagration the dancer, the actress often play important roles in world politics. Malvina Cavalazzi, the Italian *ballerina* who appeared at the Academy of Music during the Eighties and who married Charles Mapleson, son of the impressario, once told me of a part she had played in the making of United Italy. During the Austrian invasion the Italian flag was *verboten*. One night, however, during a representation of opera in a town the name of which I have forgotten, Mme. Cavalazzi wore a costume of green and white, while her male companion wore red, so that in the *pas de deux* which concluded the ballet they formed automatically a semblance of the Italian banner. The audience was raised to a hysterical pitch of enthusiasm and rushed from the theatre in a violent mood, which resulted in an immediate encounter with the Austrians and their eventual expulsion from the city.

Isadora's pantomimic interpretation of the *Marseillaise*, given in New York before the United States had entered the world war, aroused as vehement and excited an expression of enthusiasm as it would be possible for an artist to awaken in our theatre today. The audiences stood up and scarcely restrained their impatience to cheer. At the previous performances in Paris, I am told, the effect approached the incredible.... In a robe the colour of blood she stands enfolded; she sees the enemy advance; she feels the enemy as it grasps her by the throat; she kisses her flag; she tastes blood; she is all but crushed under the weight of the attack; and then she rises, triumphant, with the terrible cry, *Aux armes, citoyens!* Part of her effect is gained by gesture, part by the massing of her body, but the greater part by facial expression. In the anguished appeal she does not make a sound, beyond that made by the orchestra, but the hideous din of a hundred

raucous voices seems to ring in our ears. We see Felicien Rops's
Vengeance come to life; we see the **sans-culottes** following the
carts of the aristocrats on the way to execution ... and finally we
see the superb calm, the majestic flowing strength of the Victory of
Samothrace.... At times, legs, arms, a leg or an arm, the throat, or
the exposed breast assume an importance above that of the rest of the
mass, suggesting the unfinished sculpture of Michael Angelo, an
aposiopesis which, of course, served as Rodin's inspiration.

In the **Marche Slav** of Tschaikovsky Isadora symbolizes her conception
of the Russian moujik rising from slavery to freedom. With her hands
bound behind her back, groping, stumbling, head-bowed, knees bent, she
struggles forward, clad only in a short red garment that barely covers
her thighs. With furtive glances of extreme despair she peers above
and ahead. When the strains of **God Save the Czar** are first heard in
the orchestra she falls to her knees and you see the peasant
shuddering under the blows of the knout. The picture is a tragic one,
cumulative in its horrific details. Finally comes the moment of
release and here Isadora makes one of her great effects. She does not
spread her arms apart with a wide gesture. She brings them forward
slowly and we observe with horror that they have practically forgotten
how to move at all! They are crushed, these hands, crushed and
bleeding after their long serfdom; they are not hands at all but
claws, broken, twisted piteous claws! The expression of frightened,
almost uncomprehending, joy with which Isadora concludes the march is
another stroke of her vivid imaginative genius.

In her third number inspired by the Great War, the **Marche Lorraine**
of Louis Ganne, in which is incorporated the celebrated Chanson
Lorraine, Isadora with her pupils, symbolizes the gaiety of the
martial spirit. It is the spirit of the cavalry riding gaily with
banners waving in the wind; the infantry marching to an inspired
tune. There is nothing of the horror of war or revolution in this

picture ... only the brilliancy and dash of war ... the power and the glory!

Of late years Isadora has danced (in the conventional meaning of the word) less and less. Since her performance at Carnegie Hall several years ago of the **Liebestod** from **Tristan**, which Walter Damrosch hailed as an extremely interesting experiment, she has attempted to express something more than the joy of melody and rhythm. Indeed on at least three occasions she has danced a Requiem at the Metropolitan Opera House.... If the new art at its best is not dancing, neither is it wholly allied to the art of pantomime. It would seem, indeed, that Isadora is attempting to express something of the spirit of sculpture, perhaps what Vachell Lindsay describes as "moving sculpture." Her medium, of necessity, is still rhythmic gesture, but its development seems almost dream-like. More than the dance this new art partakes of the fluid and unending quality of music. Like any other new art it is not to be understood at first and I confess in the beginning it said nothing to me but eventually I began to take pleasure in watching it. Now Isadora's poetic and imaginative interpretation of the symphonic interlude from Cesar Franck's **Redemption** is full of beauty and meaning to me and during the whole course of its performance the interpreter scarcely rises from her knees. The neck, the throat, the shoulders, the head and arms are her means of expression. I thought of Barbey d'Aurevilly's phrase, "Elle avait l'air de monter vers Dieu les mains toutes pleines de bonnes oeuvres."

     *   *   *   *   *

Isadora's teaching has had its results but her influence has been wider in other directions. Fokine thanks her for the new Russian Ballet. She did indeed free the Russians from the conventions of the classic ballet and but for her it is doubtful if we should have seen **Scheherazade** and **Cleopatre**. **Daphnis et Chloe**, **Narcisse**, and

L'Apresmidi d'un Faune bear her direct stamp. This then, aside from her own appearances, has been her great work. Of her celebrated school of dancing I cannot speak with so much enthusiasm. The defect in her method of teaching is her insistence (consciously or unconsciously) on herself as a model. The seven remaining girls of her school dance delightfully. They are, in addition, young and beautiful, but they are miniature Isadoras. They add nothing to her style; they make the same gestures; they take the same steps; they have almost, if not quite, acquired a semblance of her spirit. They vibrate with intention; they have force; but constantly they suggest just what they are ...
imitations. When they dance alone they often make a very charming but scarcely overpowering effect. When they dance with Isadora they are but a moving row of shadow shapes of Isadora that come and go. Her own presence suffices to make the effect they all make together.... I have been told that when Isadora watches her girls dance she often weeps, for then and then only she can behold herself. One of the griefs of an actor or a dancer is that he can never see himself. This oversight of nature Isadora has to some extent overcome.

Those who like to see pretty dancing, pretty girls, pretty things in general will not find much pleasure in contemplating the art of Isadora. She is not pretty; her dancing is not pretty. She has been cast in nobler mould and it is her pleasure to climb higher mountains. Her gesture is titanic; her mood generally one of imperious grandeur. She has grown larger with the years--and by this I mean something more than the physical meaning of the word, for she is indeed heroic in build. But this is the secret of her power and force. There is no suggestion of flabbiness about her and so she can impart to us the soul of the struggling moujik, the spirit of a nation, the figure on the prow of a Greek bark.... And when she interprets the *Marseillaise* she seems indeed to feel the mighty moment.

July 14, 1917.

IV

Margaret Anglin Produces
As You Like It

Of all the comedies of Shakespeare *As You Like It* is the one which
has attracted to itself the most attention from actresses. No feminine
star but what at one time or another has a desire to play Rosalind.
Bernard Shaw says, "Who ever failed or could fail as Rosalind?" and I
am inclined to think him right, though opinions differ. It would seem,
however, that Rosalind is to the dramatic stage what Mimi in La
Boheme is to the lyric, a role in which a maximum of effect can be
gotten with a minimum of effort.

Opinions differ however. Stung to fury by Mrs. Kendal's playing of the
part, George Moore says somewhere, "Mrs. Kendal nurses children all
day and strives to play Rosalind at night. What infatuation, what
ridiculous endeavour! To realize the beautiful woodland passion and
the idea of the transformation a woman must have sinned, for only
through sin may we learn the charm of innocence. To play Rosalind a
woman must have had more than one lover, and if she has been made to
wait in the rain and has been beaten she will have done a great deal
to qualify herself for the part." Still another critic considers the
role a difficult one. He says: "With the exception of Lady Macbeth no
woman in Shakespeare is so much in controversy as Rosalind. The
character is thought to be almost unattainable. An ideal that is lofty
but at the same time vague seems to possess the Shakespeare scholar,
accompanied by the profound conviction that it never can be fulfilled.

Only a few actresses have obtained recognition as Rosalind, chief among them being Mrs. Pritchard, Peg Woffington, Mrs. Dancer, Dora Jordan, Louisa Nesbitt, Helen Faucit, Ellen Tree, Adelaide Neilson, Mrs. Scott-Siddons and Miss Mary Anderson."

Of those who have recently played Rosalind perhaps Mary Anderson, Ada Rehan, Henrietta Crosman and Julia Marlowe will remain longest in the memory, although Marie Wainwright, Mary Shaw, Mrs. Langtry and Julia Neilson are among a long list of those who have tried the part. Miss Rehan appeared in the role when Augustin Daly revived the comedy at Daly's Theatre, December 17, 1889. We are told that an effort was made in this production to emphasize the buoyant gaiety of the piece. The scenery displayed the woods embellished in a springtime green, and the acting did away as much as possible with any of the underlying melancholy which flows through the comedy.

William Winter frankly asserts--perhaps not unwittingly giving a staggering blow to the art of acting in so doing--that the reason Rosalind is not more often embodied "in a competent and enthralling manner is that her enchanting quality is something that cannot be assumed--it must be possessed; it must exist in the fibre of the individual, and its expression will then be spontaneous. Art can accomplish much, but it cannot supply the inherent captivation that constitutes the puissance of Rosalind. Miss Rehan possesses that quality, and the method of her art was the fluent method of natural grace."

Fie and a fig for Mr. Moore's theory about being beaten and standing in the rain, implies Mr. Winter!

To Mr. Winter I am also indebted for a description of Mary Anderson in *As You Like It*: "Miss Anderson, superbly handsome as Rosalind, indicated that beneath her pretty swagger, nimble satire and silver playfulness Rosalind is as earnest of Juliet--though different in temperament and mind--as fond as Viola and as constant as Imogen."

Miss Marlowe's Rosalind, somewhat along the same lines as Miss Anderson's, and Miss Crosman's, a hoydenish, tomboy sort of creature, first cousin to Mistress Nell and the young lady of *The Amazons*, should be familiar to theatregoers of the last two decades.

Last Monday evening Margaret Anglin exposed her version of the comedy. As might have been expected, it has met with some unfavourable criticism. Preconceived notions of Rosalind are as prevalent as preconceived notions of Hamlet. And yet if *As You Like It* had been produced Monday night as a "new fantastic comedy," just as *Prunella* was, for instance, I am inclined to think that everybody who dissented would have been at Miss Anglin's charming heels.

The scenery has been given undue prominence both by the management and by the writers for the newspapers. Its most interesting feature is the arrangement by which it is speedily changed about. There were no long waits caused by the settings of scenes during the acts. To say, however, that it has anything to do with the art of Gordon Craig is to speak nonsense. The scenes are painted in much the same manner as that to which we are accustomed and inured. There is a certain haze over the trees, caused partially by the tints and partially by the lighting, which produces a rather charming effect, but the outlines of the trees are quite definite; no impressionism here.

The acting is quite a different matter. *As You Like It* is one of the most modern in spirit of the Shakespeare plays. This air of modernity is still further emphasized by the fact that the play, for the most part, is written in prose. I feel certain that Bernard Shaw derived part of his inspiration for *Man and Superman* from *As You Like It*. Only in Shakespeare's play Ann Whitefield (Rosalind) pursues Octavius

(Orlando) instead of Jack Tanner. I am inclined to believe that Shaw's psychology in this instance is the more sound. It seems incredible that a girl so witty, so beautiful, and so intelligent as Rosalind should waste so much time on that sentimental, uncomprehending creature known as Orlando. Every line of Orlando should have sounded the knell of his fate in her ears. However, it must be remembered that Orlando was young and good-looking, and that, at least in the play, men of the right stamp seemed to be scarce. Of course, it is out of Touchstone that Shaw has evolved his Jack Tanner.

Whether Miss Anglin had this idea in mind or not when she produced the comedy I have no means of ascertaining. It is not essential to my point. At least she has emphasized it, and she has done the most intelligent stage directing that I have observed in the performance of a Shakespeare play for many a long season. There is consistency in the acting. Rosalind, Jaques, Touchstone, Celia, Oliver, the dukes, Charles, Sylvius, the whole lot, in fact, are natural in method and manner. There is no striving for the fantastic. Let that part of the comedy take care of itself, undoubtedly suggested Miss Anglin.

Jaques, finely portrayed by Fuller Mellish, delivers that arrant bit of nonsense "The Seven Ages of Man" in such a manner as a man might tell a rather serious story in a drawing room. "The Seven Ages of Man," of course, is just as much of an aria as *La Donna e Mobile*. It always awakens applause, but this time the applause was deserved. Mr. Mellish emphasized the cynical side of the role. He smiled in and out of season, and his most "melancholy" remarks were delivered in such a manner as to indicate that they were not too deeply felt. Jaques was a little bored with the forest and his companions, but he would have been quite in his element at Mme. Recamier's. Such was the impression that Fuller Mellish gave. Bravo, Mr. Mellish, for an impression!

Similarly the Touchstone of Sidney Greenstreet. We are accustomed to more physically attractive Touchstones, fools with finer bodies, and yet this keen-minded, stout person spoke his lines with such pertness and spontaneity that they rarely failed of their proper effect. As for Orlando, it seemed to me that Pedro de Cordoba was a little too rhetorical at times to fit in with the spirit of the performance, but Orlando at times does not fit into the play. For instance, when he utters those incredible lines:

> "If ever you have looked on better days,
> If ever been where bells have knolled to church,
> If ever sat at any good man's feast,
> If ever from your eyelids wiped a tear...."

I do not know whether Miss Anglin is a disciple of George Moore or William Winter in her acting of Rosalind. How she acquired her charm is not for us to seek into. It is only for us to credit her with having it in great plenty. A charming natural manner which made the masquerading lady seem more than a fantasy. Her warning to Phebe,

"Sell when you can; you are not for all markets,"

was delicious in its effect. I remember no Rosalind who wooed her Orlando so delightfully. For Rosalind, as Woman the Pursuer, driven forward by the Life Force, is convincingly Miss Anglin's conception--a conception which fits the comedy admirably.

As to the objections which have been raised to Miss Anglin's assumption of the masculine garments without any attempt at counterfeiting masculinity, I would ask my reader, if she be a woman, what she would do if she found it necessary to wear men's clothes. If she were not an actress she would undoubtedly behave much as she did in women's, suppressing unnecessary and telltale gestures as much as possible, but not trying to imitate mannish gestures which would immediately stamp her an impostor. There is no internal evidence in Shakespeare's play to prove that Rosalind was an actress. She might have appeared in private theatricals at the palace, but even that is doubtful. Consequently when she donned men's clothes it became evident to her that many men are effeminate in gesture and those that are do not ordinarily affect mannish movements. Her most obvious concealment was to be natural--quite herself. This, I think, is one of the most interesting and well-thought-out points of Miss Anglin's interpretation.

March 20, 1914.

The Modern Composers at a Glance

The Modern Composers at a Glance

An Impertinent Catalogue

IGOR STRAVINSKY: Paul Revere rides in Russia.

CYRIL SCOTT: A young man playing Debussy in a Maidenhead villa.

BALILLA PRATELLA: Pretty noises in funny places.

ENGELBERT HUMPERDINCK: His master's voice.

LEO ORNSTEIN: A small boy upsetting a push-cart.

GIACOMO PUCCINI: Pinocchio in a passion.

ERIK SATIE: A mandarin with a toy pistol firing into a wedding cake.

PAUL DUKAS: A giant eating bonbons.

RICCARDO ZANDONAI: Brocade dipped in garlic.

ERICH KORNGOLD: The white hope.

ARNOLD SCHOENBERG: Six times six is thirty-six--and six is ninety-two!

MAURICE RAVEL: Tomorrow ... and tomorrow ... and tomorrow....

CLAUDE DEBUSSY: Chantecler crows *pianissimo* in whole tones.

RICHARD STRAUSS: An ostrich *not* hiding his head.

SIR EDWARD ELGAR: The footman leaves his accordion in the bishop's carriage.

ITALO MONTEMEZZI: Three Kings--but no aces.

PERCY ALDRIDGE GRAINGER: An effete Australian chewing tobacco.

August 8, 1917.

    *   *   *   *   *

Notes:

[Note 1: One evidence of this is that his works are eagerly sought after and treated tenderly by the second-hand book-sellers. Some of them command fancy prices.]

[Note 2: For an account of Peladan see my essay on Erik Satie in "Interpreters and Interpretations."]

[Note 3: You will find an account of Balzac's interesting theory regarding names and letters, which may well have had a direct influence on Edgar Saltus, in Saltus's "Balzac," p. 29 *et seq.* For a precisely contrary theory turn to "The Naming of Streets" in Max Beerbohm's "Yet Again."]

[Note 4: "Wit and Wisdom from Edgar Saltus" by G. F. Monkshood and George Gamble, and "The Cynic's Posy," a collection of epigrams, the majority of which are taken from Saltus, may be brought forward in evidence.]

[Note 5: Certain books by Edgar Saltus have been announced from time to time but have never appeared; these include: "Annochiatura," "Immortal Greece," "Our Lady of Beauty," "Cimmeria," "Daughters of Dream," "Scaffolds and Altars," "Prince Charming," and "The Crimson Curtain."]

[Note 6: Houghton, Mifflin and Co,; 1884. Reprinted 1887 and 1890.]

[Note 7: Houghton, Mifflin and Co.; 1885. Reprinted by the Belford Co.]

[Note 8: George J. Coombes; 1886. Reprinted by Brentano's.]

[Note 9: Scribner and Welford; 1887. Revised edition, Belford, Clarke and Co.; 1889.]

[Note 10: Brentano's; 1887.]

[Note 11: Benjamin and Bell; 1887.]

[Note 12: Belford Co.; 1888.]

[Note 13: Belford, Clarke and Co.; 1888.]

[Note 14: Belford Co.; 1889.]

[Note 15: Belford Co.; 1889.]

[Note 16: Belford, Clarke and Co.; 1889.]

[Note 17: Belford Co.; 1890.]

[Note 18: Belford Co.; 1891.]

[Note 19: Belford Co.; 1891. Reprinted by Mitchell Kennerley; 1906.]

[Note 20: P. F. Collier; 1892; "Written especially for 'Once a Week Library.'"]

[Note 21: Morrill, Higgins and Co;. 1893. Reprinted by Mitchell Kennerley; 1906.]

[Note 22: F. Tennyson Neely; 1893.]

[Note 23: Tudor Press: 1894.]

[Note 24: The Transatlantic Publishing Co.; 1895.]

[Note 25: Ainslee; 1903.]

[Note 26: A. Wessels Co.; 1905.]

[Note 27: Mitchell Kennerley; 1906.]

[Note 28: J. B. Lippincott Co.; 1906.]

[Note 29: Mitchell Kennerley; 1907.]

[Note 30: Mitchell Kennerley; 1907.]

[Note 31: Mitchell Kennerley; 1909.]

[Note 32: Pulitzer Publishing Co.; 1912.]

[Note 33: In an essay entitled "The Great American Composer" in my book, "Interpreters and Interpretations."]

*   *   *   *   *

The Codes Of Hammurabi And Moses
W. W. Davies

QTY

The discovery of the Hammurabi Code is one of the greatest achievements of archaeology, and is of paramount interest, not only to the student of the Bible, but also to all those interested in ancient history...

Religion   **ISBN:** *1-59462-338-4*   **Pages:132**

MSRP $12.95

The Theory of Moral Sentiments
Adam Smith

QTY

This work from 1749. contains original theories of conscience amd moral judgment and it is the foundation for systemof morals.

Philosophy   ISBN: *1-59462-777-0*   **Pages:536**

MSRP $19.95

Jessica's First Prayer
Hesba Stretton

QTY

In a screened and secluded corner of one of the many railway-bridges which span the streets of London there could be seen a few years ago, from five o'clock every morning until half past eight, a tidily set-out coffee-stall, consisting of a trestle and board, upon which stood two large tin cans, with a small fire of charcoal burning under each so as to keep the coffee boiling during the early hours of the morning when the work-people were thronging into the city on their way to their daily toil...

Pages:84

Childrens   ISBN: *1-59462-373-2*   *MSRP $9.95*

My Life and Work
Henry Ford

QTY

Henry Ford revolutionized the world with his implementation of mass production for the Model T automobile. Gain valuable business insight into his life and work with his own auto-biography... "We have only started on our development of our country we have not as yet, with all our talk of wonderful progress, done more than scratch the surface. The progress has been wonderful enough but..."

Pages:300

Biographies/   ISBN: *1-59462-198-5*   *MSRP $21.95*

www.bookjungle.com *email: sales@bookjungle.com fax: 630-214-0564 mail: Book Jungle PO Box 2226 Champaign, IL 61825*

The Art of Cross-Examination
Francis Wellman

QTY

I presume it is the experience of every author, after his first book is published upon an important subject, to be almost overwhelmed with a wealth of ideas and illustrations which could readily have been included in his book, and which to his own mind, at least, seem to make a second edition inevitable. Such certainly was the case with me; and when the first edition had reached its sixth impression in five months, I rejoiced to learn that it seemed to my publishers that the book had met with a sufficiently favorable reception to justify a second and considerably enlarged edition. ..

Reference   ISBN: *1-59462-647-2*

Pages:412

MSRP $19.95

On the Duty of Civil Disobedience
Henry David Thoreau

QTY

Thoreau wrote his famous essay, On the Duty of Civil Disobedience, as a protest against an unjust but popular war and the immoral but popular institution of slave-owning. He did more than write—he declined to pay his taxes,   and was hauled off to gaol in consequence. Who can say how much this refusal of his hastened the end of the war and of slavery ?

Law   ISBN: *1-59462-747-9*

Pages:48

MSRP $7.45

Dream Psychology Psychoanalysis for Beginners
Sigmund Freud

QTY

Sigmund Freud, born Sigismund Schlomo Freud (May 6, 1856 - September 23, 1939), was a Jewish-Austrian neurologist and psychiatrist who co-founded the psychoanalytic school of psychology. Freud is best known for his theories of the unconscious mind, especially involving the mechanism of repression; his redefinition of sexual desire as mobile and directed towards a wide variety of objects; and his therapeutic techniques, especially his understanding of transference in the therapeutic relationship and the presumed value of dreams as sources of insight into unconscious desires.

Psychology   ISBN: *1-59462-905-6*

Pages:196

MSRP $15.45

The Miracle of Right Thought
Orison Swett Marden

QTY

Believe with all of your heart that you will do what you were made to do. When the mind has once formed the habit of holding cheerful, happy, prosperous pictures, it will not be easy to form the opposite habit. It does not matter how improbable or how far away this realization may see, or how dark the prospects may be, if we visualize them as best we can, as vividly as possible, hold tenaciously to them and vigorously struggle to attain them, they will gradually become actualized, realized in the life. But a desire, a longing without endeavor, a yearning abandoned or held indifferently will vanish without realization.

Self Help   ISBN: *1-59462-644-8*

Pages:360

MSRP $25.45

The Rosicrucian Cosmo-Conception Mystic Christianity *by Max Heindel*　ISBN: *1-59462-188-8*　**$38.95**
The Rosicrucian Cosmo-conception is not dogmatic, neither does it appeal to any other authority than the reason of the student. It is: not controversial, but is: sent forth in the, hope that it may help to clear...　New Age/Religion Pages 646

Abandonment To Divine Providence *by Jean-Pierre de Caussade*　ISBN: *1-59462-228-0*　**$25.95**
"The Rev. Jean Pierre de Caussade was one of the most remarkable spiritual writers of the Society of Jesus in France in the 18th Century. His death took place at Toulouse in 1751. His works have gone through many editions and have been republished...　Inspirational/Religion Pages 400

Mental Chemistry *by Charles Haanel*　ISBN: *1-59462-192-6*　**$23.95**
Mental Chemistry allows the change of material conditions by combining and appropriately utilizing the power of the mind. Much like applied chemistry creates something new and unique out of careful combinations of chemicals the mastery of mental chemistry...　New Age Pages 354

The Letters of Robert Browning and Elizabeth Barret Barrett 1845-1846 vol II　ISBN: *1-59462-193-4*　**$35.95**
by Robert Browning and Elizabeth Barrett　Biographies Pages 596

Gleanings In Genesis (volume I) *by Arthur W. Pink*　ISBN: *1-59462-130-6*　**$27.45**
Appropriately has Genesis been termed "the seed plot of the Bible" for in it we have, in germ form, almost all of the great doctrines which are afterwards fully developed in the books of Scripture which follow...　Religion/Inspirational Pages 420

The Master Key *by L. W. de Laurence*　ISBN: *1-59462-001-6*　**$30.95**
In no branch of human knowledge has there been a more lively increase of the spirit of research during the past few years than in the study of Psychology, Concentration and Mental Discipline. The requests for authentic lessons in Thought Control, Mental Discipline and...　New Age/Business Pages 422

The Lesser Key Of Solomon Goetia *by L. W. de Laurence*　ISBN: *1-59462-092-X*　**$9.95**
This translation of the first book of the "Lemegton" which is now for the first time made accessible to students of Talismanic Magic was done, after careful collation and edition, from numerous Ancient Manuscripts in Hebrew, Latin, and French...　New Age/Occult Pages 92

Rubaiyat Of Omar Khayyam *by Edward Fitzgerald*　ISBN:*1-59462-332-5*　**$13.95**
Edward Fitzgerald, whom the world has already learned, in spite of his own efforts to remain within the shadow of anonymity, to look upon as one of the rarest poets of the century, was born at Bredfield, in Suffolk, on the 31st of March, 1809. He was the third son of John Purcell...　Music Pages 172

Ancient Law *by Henry Maine*　ISBN: *1-59462-128-4*　**$29.95**
The chief object of the following pages is to indicate some of the earliest ideas of mankind, as they are reflected in Ancient Law, and to point out the relation of those ideas to modern thought.　Religiom/History Pages 452

Far-Away Stories *by William J. Locke*　ISBN: *1-59462-129-2*　**$19.45**
"Good wine needs no bush, but a collection of mixed vintages does. And this book is just such a collection. Some of the stories I do not want to remain buried for ever in the museum files of dead magazine-numbers an author's not unpardonable vanity..."　Fiction Pages 272

Life of David Crockett *by David Crockett*　ISBN: *1-59462-250-7*　**$27.45**
"Colonel David Crockett was one of the most remarkable men of the times in which he lived. Born in humble life, but gifted with a strong will, an indomitable courage, and unremitting perseverance...　Biographies/New Age Pages 424

Lip-Reading *by Edward Nitchie*　ISBN: *1-59462-206-X*　**$25.95**
Edward B. Nitchie, founder of the New York School for the Hard of Hearing, now the Nitchie School of Lip-Reading, Inc, wrote "LIP-READING Principles and Practice". The development and perfecting of this meritorious work on lip-reading was an undertaking...　How-to Pages 400

A Handbook of Suggestive Therapeutics, Applied Hypnotism, Psychic Science　ISBN: *1-59462-214-0*　**$24.95**
by Henry Munro　Health/New Age/Health/Self-help Pages 376

A Doll's House: and Two Other Plays *by Henrik Ibsen*　ISBN: *1-59462-112-8*　**$19.95**
Henrik Ibsen created this classic when in revolutionary 1848 Rome. Introducing some striking concepts in playwriting for the realist genre, this play has been studied the world over.　Fiction/Classics/Plays 308

The Light of Asia *by sir Edwin Arnold*　ISBN: *1-59462-204-3*　**$13.95**
In this poetic masterpiece, Edwin Arnold describes the life and teachings of Buddha. The man who was to become known as Buddha to the world was born as Prince Gautama of India but he rejected the worldly riches and abandoned the reigns of power when...　Religion/History/Biographies Pages 170

The Complete Works of Guy de Maupassant *by Guy de Maupassant*　ISBN: *1-59462-157-8*　**$16.95**
"For days and days, nights and nights, I had dreamed of that first kiss which was to consecrate our engagement, and I knew not on what spot I should put my lips..."　Fiction/Classics Pages 240

The Art of Cross-Examination *by Francis L. Wellman*　ISBN: *1-59462-309-0*　**$26.95**
Written by a renowned trial lawyer, Wellman imparts his experience and uses case studies to explain how to use psychology to extract desired information through questioning.　How-to/Science/Reference Pages 408

Answered or Unanswered? *by Louisa Vaughan*　ISBN: *1-59462-248-5*　**$10.95**
Miracles of Faith in China　Religion Pages 112

The Edinburgh Lectures on Mental Science (1909) *by Thomas*　ISBN: *1-59462-008-3*　**$11.95**
This book contains the substance of a course of lectures recently given by the writer in the Queen Street Hall, Edinburgh. Its purpose is to indicate the Natural Principles governing the relation between Mental Action and Material Conditions...　New Age/Psychology Pages 148

Ayesha *by H. Rider Haggard*　ISBN: *1-59462-301-5*　**$24.95**
Verily and indeed it is the unexpected that happens! Probably if there was one person upon the earth from whom the Editor of this, and of a certain previous history, did not expect to hear again...　Classics Pages 380

Ayala's Angel *by Anthony Trollope*　ISBN: *1-59462-352-X*　**$29.95**
The two girls were both pretty, but Lucy who was twenty-one who supposed to be simple and comparatively unattractive, whereas Ayala was credited, as her Bombwhat romantic name might show, with poetic charm and a taste for romance. Ayala when her father died was nineteen...　Fiction Pages 484

The American Commonwealth *by James Bryce*　ISBN: *1-59462-286-8*　**$34.45**
An interpretation of American democratic political theory. It examines political mechanics and society from the perspective of Scotsman James Bryce　Politics Pages 572

Stories of the Pilgrims *by Margaret P. Pumphrey*　ISBN: *1-59462-116-0*　**$17.95**
This book explores pilgrims religious oppression in England as well as their escape to Holland and eventual crossing to America on the Mayflower, and their early days in New England...　History Pages 268

QTY

The Fasting Cure *by Sinclair Upton*   ISBN: *1-59462-222-1* **$13.95**
*In the Cosmopolitan Magazine for May, 1910, and in the Contemporary Review (London) for April, 1910, I published an article dealing with my experi-
ences in fasting. I have written a great many magazine articles, but never one which attracted so much attention...* New Age/Self Help/Health Pages 164

Hebrew Astrology *by Sepharial*   ISBN: *1-59462-308-2* **$13.45**
*In these days of advanced thinking it is a matter of common observation that we have left many of the old landmarks behind and that we are now pressing
forward to greater heights and to a wider horizon than that which represented the mind-content of our progenitors...* Astrology Pages 144

Thought Vibration or The Law of Attraction in the Thought World   ISBN: *1-59462-127-6* **$12.95**

by William Walker Atkinson   Psychology/Religion Pages 144

Optimism *by Helen Keller*   ISBN: *1-59462-108-X* **$15.95**
*Helen Keller was blind, deaf, and mute since 19 months old, yet famously learned how to overcome these handicaps, communicate with the world, and
spread her lectures promoting optimism. An inspiring read for everyone...* Biographies/Inspirational Pages 84

Sara Crewe *by Frances Burnett*   ISBN: *1-59462-360-0* **$9.45**
*In the first place, Miss Minchin lived in London. Her home was a large, dull, tall one, in a large, dull square, where all the houses were alike, and all the
sparrows were alike, and where all the door-knockers made the same heavy sound...* Childrens/Classic Pages 88

The Autobiography of Benjamin Franklin *by Benjamin Franklin*   ISBN: *1-59462-135-7* **$24.95**
*The Autobiography of Benjamin Franklin has probably been more extensively read than any other American historical work, and no other book of its kind
has had such ups and downs of fortune. Franklin lived for many years in England, where he was agent...* Biographies/History Pages 332

Name	
Email	
Telephone	
Address	
City, State ZIP	

☐ **Credit Card**   ☐ **Check / Money Order**

Credit Card Number	
Expiration Date	
Signature	

*Please Mail to: Book Jungle
PO Box 2226
Champaign, IL 61825*
or Fax to: 630-214-0564

ORDERING INFORMATION
web: *www.bookjungle.com*
email: *sales@bookjungle.com*
fax: *630-214-0564*
mail: *Book Jungle PO Box 2226 Champaign, IL 61825*
or PayPal *to sales@bookjungle.com*

Please contact us for bulk discounts

DIRECT-ORDER TERMS

**20% Discount if You Order
Two or More Books**
Free Domestic Shipping!
Accepted: Master Card, Visa,
Discover, American Express